Bertie was in ___ of losing his perspective...

A monkey was telling the creation story to American capitalists in the fantasy camp of their lost childhood.

"I created them in my own image," the bizarre narrator continued. "Then they came down from the trees and befouled the land with their filth. Worst of all, they began to think for themselves, and forgot their original purpose, which was to GLORIFY ME."

With a guttural roar the ape threw itself against the door of its cage. The grown men screamed like little boys and fell over one another. The eloquent ape resumed its tirade.

"YOU! YOU BETRAYED ME! My power is gone. But in your arrogance you will destroy yourselves. You think that you can create with machines that which I became a god to do. Here is my prophecy: YOU WILL ALL DIE!" The monkey abruptly threw off its cap and robes and screamed in gibberish. It had reverted completely to an animal state.

The camp leader reappeared from the shadows. "That's your scary horror story for tonight, campers. Let's all go to our tents now. There's cocoa and cookies for everybody."

■　　　■　　　■

"The spirit of Kafka is rejuvenated in this wonderfully bizarre, charmingly antic first novel by a talent to watch."
—Harlan Ellison

"A funny, original, and poignant treatment of the nuclear issue."
—Marty Asher,
author of *Shelter*

The AMERICAN BOOK of the DEAD

STEPHEN BILLIAS

POPULAR LIBRARY

An Imprint of Warner Books, Inc.

A Warner Communications Company

POPULAR LIBRARY EDITION

Copyright © 1987 by Stephen Billias

Popular Library®, the fanciful P design, and Questar® are registered
trademarks of Warner Books, Inc.

Cover illustration by Gary Ruddell

Popular Library books are published by
Warner Books, Inc.
666 Fifth Avenue
New York, N.Y. 10103

 A Warner Communications Company

Printed in the United States of America

First Printing: May, 1987

10 9 8 7 6 5 4 3 2 1

For Laura and Jonathan
May they live to see this book not come true

In a region of celestial
grandeur far removed from
human vision, Mahatma Gandhi
sat on a cosmic cloud.
Gently, tirelessly, he wove
sparkling strands for
Indra's Net, which connects
each thing in the universe
to every other thing. As he spun,
he wept for the people of Earth.

Table of Contents

1

How the ComputerPaper Got Its Stripes

Bertie Rupp wanted to be a farmer. His father was a farmer, and his father's father and all the fathers before that were farmers too. Every day Bertie went to the land. There's more to farm work than tending fields: there are cows to milk and wood to chop and tools to mend and endless other tasks, but most of all, the crop has to be raised. Bertie's family grew corn.

The Rupps all lived together. They ate a lot of corn. Uncle Buddy swore that heaven was fresh corn right off the stalk tossed into a waiting pot of boiling water. He wouldn't get an argument from the rest of the Rupps, except maybe from Granma Rupp, who had no teeth. She ate her corn mashed with warm milk.

In the fields Bertie followed his father back and forth across the furrows. He lived as deeply in the cycle of the seasons as any other animal. In the early spring he took a stick and banged at the frozen clods of dirt his father turned up. Later mud slithered through his toes while rains filled the rows between young green shoots.

During the summer he lay on his back on the warm earth and watched hawks spinning slowly in the sky far and high above him, or he ran, shaded, through tall rows of corn that were to him like a mysterious forest, even though he knew their limits precisely and had seen them grow with his own eyes.

Harvest was the best of times, when the corn fell before the harvester and the flat land was again revealed. Then Bertie explored the leavings and trailings of the cutting and played among the stubble and stalks. In short, Bertie lived in Paradise, Indiana.

One day a man from the city came to the Rupp place. Ma and Pa Rupp were sitting on the porch. (It was Sunday.) The man offered them a whole lot of money for the farm. Pa Rupp didn't want to take it because he knew that the land was everything, that money was nothing. But Ma Rupp had a sister in Chicago who said that living was easy in the big city as long as you had money, so they sold the farm and off they went.

Bertie was miserable. He missed his fields. The noisy crowds of the city scared him. He stayed home a lot, and he became a quiet boy. Only at school did he find any happiness. His new teachers were much smarter than the old woman at the country school. They taught him the secrets of mathematics.

Before Pa Rupp shriveled up like a dried-out old corn husk and died, he told Bertie: "Numbers aren't real, cities aren't real. Corn is real. Land. And corn." Bertie didn't understand this until he discovered imaginary numbers.

Bertie was a genius. He graduated from college a year early, earned his Ph.D. in one year, and went out into the world of business. Bertie's head was filled with matrices, logarithms, and abstruse equations and calculations, but inside him was still a little boy who had roamed godlike over fifteen acres of Indiana farmland.

Bertie got a job with IBM. Everybody wore white shirts there. Everybody wore skinny black ties there. Everybody was the same there. Bertie worked on the early IBM machines. In fact, his mind was the basis for the modern-day computer, so neatly laid out in rows, so linear, so Indiana-square and flat. When the first roll printers were introduced, it was Bertie who looked at the continuous white sheet and said: "Put stripes on it. Give them something to follow." Of course, it worked, and ever since then, computer printouts have had blue or green stripes. IBM made lots of money but not Bertie.

After this contribution Bertie's career at IBM disintegrated. In the annals of the company and of history, Bertie Rupp is trivialized as the man who put stripes on readout, but this story starts when, Bertie, knowing that the world was about to destroy itself, went insane.

The clinical term for his illness is nucleomitophobia: an unnatural fear of being blown up by nuclear weapons. Bertie thought it was a natural and reasonable fear, and when his prefabricated fellows at IBM disagreed, hc was stunned. His neurosis manifested itself in this manner: He began to search for himself. By doing so, he took the first great step toward healing, and Enlightenment, and the Book.

2

Growing the Bonsai Sequoia

Life got tough for Bertie. His prescient knowledge obsessed him. The pain he felt, the future pain, consumed his thoughts. He behaved like a mad Old Testament prophet, boring and depressing everyone he talked to with his dire ravings. Hoping for a new start, he left his job at IBM and moved across the country to San Francisco.

Bertie reduced himself to a monkish life-style, passing quickly through various stages of poverty and asceticism. He became a vegetarian. He smoked marijuana until his eyes turned the color of sand on Mars. He drank his way down the social structure until he found people like himself, people who agreed with him. But they were staggering drunk and shitting in the gutters between parked automobiles. What could they do about *it*?

In the extreme of despair, Bertie was struck by a spiritual impulse. For him, as for so many people, the inner life was an escape. Bertie hoped somehow to survive the war by hiding within himself. His new fervor gave some discipline to his life; he settled into a fairly regular routine: temporary office jobs with little responsibility combined with long hours of meditation. He wandered through corporations where he might have been a manager; now he was reduced to making and filing copies of other people's work.

Finally the heavens stopped swimming, and voices lost their faraway ringing echo in his ear, and faces no longer shimmered before him. Meditation slowed the chaotic charge of his rampant mind. He was able to focus once again, though the knowledge of the coming apocalypse pressed on him continually.

For Bertie, meditation was like the moment just after the harvest, like a sigh, the smooth dying-down of it. He often sat in deep reverie and let the Great Stillness pass into him and become him.

Although Bertie lived in the city now, he retained a love for growing things. He talked to his plants and played them his favorite music. He lost himself in their slow stages of growth, blossom, and decay. One day a tiny newspaper ad attracted his attention:

Bonsai on Exhibit

in

Japantown

at

The Temple of Great Restraint

Bertie went dressed in his current style: a pair of Japanese straw sandals, pajama pants, a camouflage jacket, a white shirt with skinny black tie, a polka-dot banzai headband, and mirrored sunglasses.

He was welcomed at the temple door by shaven-headed monks in flowing saffron robes. A cross section of San Francisco society crowded the building's main hall where the plants were displayed. Ordinarily, at an event like this, people watched each other as at art exhibits or theater openings, but here the plants were so spectacular that they were the center of attention, as they were intended to be. They were fantastically expensive. The cheapest, a tiny maple at the height of its autumn foliage, littering its pedestal with dainty leaves of crimson, orange, and scarlet, cost a thousand dollars.

There were dwarf cedars and birches and fruit-bearing species with perfect miniature oranges and avocados. In the background a tape played the extended, low basso moaning of the long Japanese flute, the *shakuhachi*, an instrument mastered only by priests, half sung and full of guttural utterances, so that the musician made his voice and his flute blend together, like jazz musicians sometimes do.

Bertie had wandered all the way to the back of the exhibit when a voice startled him by clearly addressing him.

"So, it's you?"

"What?" Bertie strained to focus on the source of the voice. He was bad at this direct human contact.

"Aren't you?" There—oh, God—it was the head priest talking to him. Although he wore no outward sign of his rank, Bertie could tell the man's position by his imposing presence.

"Well, I guess so," said Bertie rather unconvincingly.

"Yes, we've been expecting you."

"You have?"

"Take off the glasses, please. Step in here."

Bertie did as he was told and at once found himself in a dimly lit inner room of the temple. He rubbed his eyes.

"Sometimes a wall no thicker than rice paper separates us from the Truth," the priest said, and smiled strangely at Bertie.

Arranged in four concentric circles were groups of monks sitting cross-legged in meditation. At the center of the circles was a bush, a tree. Bertie leaned closer to look at it, since everyone else in the room also seemed to be staring intently at it. All at once he saw that it was a bonsai sequoia, larger than most bonsai but only because it was the reduction of a primordial giant. It stood six feet tall.

"This is a young tree, just a sapling, perhaps only one hundred and fifty years old," the priest said.

"But, but—" Bertie sputtered, for he had some knowledge of these things, and he knew that no amount of pruning and cutting back and water deprivation would keep a great sequoia down.

"It's life force is very strong," the priest replied, answering Bertie's unasked question. "This bonsai is produced by the mental efforts of many monks. Hence, Temple of Great Restraint. Even now, as I talk to you, a portion of my mind is concentrated on the bonsai. This great mind pressure is all that keeps the tree from springing through the roof of the temple. This practice is known as the Yoga of Psychic Gravity."

Bertie looked wildly around. How did he get in here? What was going on?

"Calm yourself," the priest said. "Sit down. Cross your legs, assume the lotus position. There. Don't you feel better? You know, you've been causing quite a stir here with your ferocious chanting."

"How? I—" Bertie was left speechless. This man seemed to know all about him. It was a paranoid's worst nightmare come true.

"Your meditations, though powerful, are not pointed. It was proposed that you might like to join us here. Can you imagine the degree of concentration required?"

At last Bertie found his tongue. "If you know so much about me, you know my fear."

"Yes."

"If what I think is going to happen happens, not just me but you and that tree and this building and everything else in the city is going to be destroyed."

"Yes. That is true."

"Isn't that something to be afraid of?"

"Listen carefully." The priest sat down opposite Bertie; the two of them occupied a part of the circular space whose focus was a small, living piece of wood. "Now listen. Your fear is a common one, a justifiable one. Here is the answer, in the words of the great Yasutani Roshi of Japan: 'Become one with the Bomb and what is there to fear?'"

"But—" Bertie blurted as the priest's words instantly cleaved his mind into two parts the way a bolt of lightning splits a massive boulder without penetrating either half. One side knew what it heard to be the Truth, the other side screamed and writhed and refused to believe it.

"There is more," the Zen man continued. "He also said: 'Whether you want to or not, you will do so, anyway, so embrace it.'"

Bertie reeled and fell over on his side with his legs still crossed. The priest looked at him steadily and waited patiently while Bertie righted himself.

At last the monk spoke again. "Even though I talked and the bones in your ear vibrated, you did not hear. Too bad for you. Your road will be a long one. I'll get you on it. No, you have traveled some way already. You have discovered truths in ancient books, have you not?"

Bertie nodded. He'd studied Sanskrit. He could read the Vedic texts in the original. Sometimes on temporary jobs he confounded his coworkers with a few words spoken in the archaic language.

"Did you know, however, that there is a secret modern text which expounds the same eternal truths for people like you? Perhaps you've heard of it? *The American Book of the Dead.*"

"No" was the only word dazed Bertie could manage.

"The answers you seek are in that Book."

"Where is it? Where can I get a copy?"

Instead of answering, the priest reached in the folds of his robe and removed a shiny black sphere no larger than a marble.

"Take this."

"What is it?"

"An object for you to meditate upon. Keep it with you, you will need it."

With the priest's last words ringing in his ears, Bertie was shoved through a door into the relative brightness of the exhibit hall. He barely had time to get his legs uncrossed and drop them to the floor, so that he wobbled unsteadily for a moment while blood rushed through constricted arteries. Knowing that his interview with the temple abbot was over, Bertie began to walk away. Then he remembered his mirrored sunglasses, turned to retrieve them, and found himself facing a solid wall.

Bertie put his hands on the wall and ran them along it in disbelief, until he saw that other people were looking at him sideways. He questioned one of the robed hosts, who denied that there was any inner room or any such person as Bertie described to him and stared indifferently at the black marble Bertie offered as proof. Bertie became so insistent that he was politely asked to leave. He stormed outside in a rage, only to discover his sunglasses in one of the many pockets of his camouflage jacket.

3

The Setting
Face-to-face

During the next few weeks Bertie ravaged the bookshops of his city. He pestered book dealers and antiquarians. He canvassed the many university libraries in the area. No record of any book by that title was ever found, not even at the Library of Congress, which Bertie besieged with so many letters of inquiry that he was sent a bill for research hours.

The search for the Book consumed him. Where was the Book? Who had written it? What did it say? These questions impelled Bertie to manic heights of amateur detective work. He believed implicitly in the existence of the Book. A Zen priest would not lie to him. But had he talked to a Zen priest? Only the tangible denseness of his meditation marble kept Bertie from wondering if he had imagined the entire episode.

One week the temporary agency for which Bertie worked sent him to an insurance company. These assignments were the closest thing to hell on earth for unhappy Bertie. He loathed the repetition of the work, which consisted of inputting policies on a CRT terminal, a system which Bertie's own early genius had made possible.

Accumulated Life Assurance Company used sophisticated programming to perform its billing functions; however, it had no concept of modern office partitioning. Bertie was sent to a room as primitive as Bob Crachit's, except that the army of clerks used noisy keyboards instead of ledgers at their rows of desks. The uncarpeted floor was grimly lit by the angry glare of badly misfiring fluorescent lights. Poor Bertie—he was led to his desk and given a pile of someone else's mistakes to correct.

The only relief in the tedium of data entry came when Bertie went to make a photocopy of some particularly egregious error. As he approached the machine Bertie saw that one of the chief officers of the company was standing at the duplicator and making his own copies.

Why wasn't his secretary doing the job? Bertie wondered. He decided that the documents must be confidential company information. The man didn't know how to operate the machine and was using it incorrectly, running his copies from last page to first. Then, when he finished his copying, he made a common mistake: He took his copies and all his originals except the last sheet under the cover, still facedown on the glass.

Bertie stepped briskly up to the device and pushed the "copy" button. The mystic green light passed over the as yet unseen document. The copier gave off a fuzzy static feel as it completed the negative reversal process.

Bertie lifted the cover and removed the original, still facedown. He grabbed the copy and shoved it into his pocket before anyone saw him. Then he ran after the executive. "Sir, sir," Bertie said, but the boss did not acknowledge his presence, although Bertie was right behind him. "Sir, you left your paper in the machine," he said. The man spun around instantly. His hand shot out, and he took the original from Bertie before the frightened little temp could say another word. The man stood before Bertie and glared at him silently,

holding him in place with a look while he seemed to examine
the contents of Bertie's mind.

Bertie recognized him. He was a government employee,
at the Cabinet level, who had returned to private business
after a change of administration.

"You didn't read this, did you?" _____ _____ asked
him.

"No, sir," Bertie answered honestly. "I saw that you were
making copies by yourself, so I figured it must be private."

"What's your name?"

"Rupp. Bertram Rupp."

"That's very sharp, Rupp. I owe you one. Say, you're not
related to the German Rupps, are you?"

"My family were farmers, not industrialists," Bertie said.

"What are you doing here?"

"Just temporary work," Bertie said, and hung his head a
little.

"Well, keep it up, Rupp, and maybe we'll put you on full-
time. Heh, heh! 'Keep it up Rupp'—I like that." The big
man laughed, and still chuckling, he turned without another
look at Bertie and disappeared into inner offices Bertie would
never enter.

Though the crumpled sheet intrigued him, Bertie restrained
himself until the workday was finished and he had taken his
long bus ride home. He lived in a small apartment in an urban
neighborhood within the city limits but far from the crowded
jumble of skyscrapers downtown. His place was sparsely
furnished in the Japanese style but was overrun with plants.
Bertie's apartment was in two rooms of a Victorian home,
so that Bertie's living room was the old parlor, with enormous
triple bay windows he had given over entirely to the growing
of domestic sinsemilla marijuana. Seating consisted of cush-
ions on the floor. Bertie made himself comfortable. He removed the costume he wore to the office and donned a silk
kimono bathrobe. He sat cross-legged with a glass of guava-

banana nectar amid his diffenbachia, jade plants, ferns, and one or two vibrant bonsai.

When the nervous buzz of the day receded, Bertie got out the paper and unfolded it. He expected to find some interesting office gossip on the corporate level, or perhaps, he fantasized, something political, since _____ _____'s name still appeared on newspaper pages from time to time in connection with world events.

Instead, Bertie received the shock of his life. There before him, on a wrinkled and slightly torn copy of a copy, were the opening words to the object of Bertie's desire: the Book. He recognized it instantly. In elaborate calligraphy with swirls and serifs were the following words:

HEREIN LIETH THE SETTING FACE-TO-FACE WITH REALITY: VOID WHERE PROHIBITED

With trembling hands Bertie smoothed out the paper and laid it before him. Then he thought. He thought so hard, his face glowed like a jack-o'-lantern. He stared at the words, which were a mixture of arcane esoterica and jargon Americana. The suggestion of immense power emanated from the page. If Bertie could grasp the full meaning contained in those few words, he would be liberated.

But this was only the barest introduction to the Book, Bertie realized. He had to see more of it. He remembered how this page had come to him: the horrible temporary assignment, then the chance meeting with _____ _____ at the photocopy machine. The Book, there, in the hands of men like _____ _____. Covetousness sprang up in Bertie's heart. He must have, he would have, that *Book*!

The next day at lunchtime Bertie visited a nearby electronics store. All afternoon he watched for _____

_____, but the big man remained in seclusion in the inner
sanctum of Accumulated Life. That evening, as soon as Bertie
was home, he took an assortment of tiny screwdrivers, a
miniature soldering iron, and some fine-gauged needle-nose
pliers. With grace and precision he crafted a small black box
that contained the microchips he had purchased from the
store. When finished, it resembled a small garage-door opener
with a single white button on its otherwise smooth surface.

He had only to wait for the opportunity to use it. The
temporary job had started on Monday. Tuesday was the day
of his first contact with the Book. Wednesday he had gone
to the store. Thursday he took the device to work in his pants
pocket.

Bertie had two days. Then his work at Accumulated Life
would be finished and Bertie would be sent to work elsewhere. He had to hope that _____ _____ would make
more copies, and sure enough, at three-thirty that Thursday
afternoon the corporate giant came out of his den and ambled
toward the photocopy machine.

Bertie prepared himself. He observed that _____
_____ was about to copy only a single sheet, cautious perhaps because of his previous error. When _____
_____ pressed the button for one copy, Bertie activated his
concealed device. _____ _____ retrieved his copy and
original. As he walked away a second copy slid silently into
the auxiliary tray. Bertie sidled up to the machine and sur-
reptitiously removed the extra copy.

Later in the day, almost at closing time, Bertie managed
the same trick again—copying one more page. It seemed to
him for one terrifying instant that _____ _____ took
notice of his presence, but Bertie wasn't sure. Oh, the agony
Bertie endured. At any moment he expected to be arrested
and taken away under the stares of two hundred entry clerks.
But nothing happened.

At last Bertie was home. The scene of Tuesday night was

repeated. Bertie unfolded the two papers. The first turned out to be insurance form number 11111, a curious document that was a total disclaimer, absolving Accumulated Life Assurance Company for any claim lodged against it no matter what the circumstances. Further, this disclaimer superseded any previous forms signed between the company and any individual, corporation, or entity, from time immemorial until further notice. Bertie scratched his head and placed this paper aside.

He realized right away that the second sheet was what he had hoped for. Through the thin paper he could see the curling ciphers that resembled Sanskrit, though the words were in English. Meditating for a moment, Bertie prepared himself for the revelations.

This time he unfolded the paper and gently smoothed it before turning it over. Then he placed the paper faceup in front of him and let his mind seize the glowing words:

RADIANCE OF THE CLEAR LIGHT
OF PURE REALITY:
WHITER THAN WHITE

And beneath this a second aphorism:

CHANGELESS CHANGE, PRIMORDIAL ESSENCE
OF THE GREAT PRIMAL BEGINNING:
NEW, IMPROVED, LONGER-LASTING

Bertie's brain exploded like the controlled chaos inside a breeder reactor, creating more energy than it consumed. Bertie blustered Bertie blathered Bertie burbled Bertie bumbled about his apartment in a trancelike stupor. These passages, so vivid, so profound and incisive—what did they mean? Were they chapter headings or theses for impending elaborations, or were they self-contained epigraphs? His fervor and his lusting after the Book soared to critical mass. He resolved to break his Buddhist vow against theft. He rationalized it as liberating the Book from the hands of the capitalists. Tomorrow, he swore, he would break and enter the office of _____ _____.

Bertie woke up with a headache. The sickening green light of the CRT always gave it to him, and this was to be the fifth straight day of it. He wondered if he could endure it. Did he have the courage of a thief? It didn't seem likely, Bertie thought to himself as he looked in the mirror at the wild-eyed figure in boxer shorts and knee socks.

When he arrived at the office, he was given a particularly nasty set of idiocies to deal with. Some branch office had used temporaries to input their previous week's policies. It took Bertie the whole morning to straighten out the mess.

By noontime he had a Thorazine headache. His skin was crawling with unseen insects; his shirt was stuck to the small of his back with nervous sweat. He wanted to slink home at lunch and spend the rest of the day in bed. His corroded state of mind was completely unprepared for the terror and shock that jolted him when he saw _____ _____ striding purposefully toward his desk.

Two hundred heads around him jerked up nervously. _____ _____ stopped at Bertie's desk, towering over the little man.

"Come with me, Rupp." Bertie stood up on shaky legs and followed _____ _____. A prickly, uncomfortable sensation on the back of Bertie's neck told him of the stares of others.

Instead of entering the main offices, _____ _____ led Bertie through an exit door into the employee parking lot. Several scenarios played through Bertie's mind, all of them ending in his violent death. In _____ _____'s reserved parking spot was a beautiful antique Rolls Silver Cloud, with right-hand steering wheel and a deluxe mahogany interior.

"Rupp, I took a look at your employment records, and it says there that you can drive this thing. Is that so?"

It was. What lousy manual labor had Bertie not performed in his wanderings since the days at IBM? He had been chauffeur, taxi driver, kitchen worker. But where had _____ _____ gotten his résumé? He must have called the temp agency.

"Yes, I can, but—"

"Good," _____ _____ said, interrupting him. "My man has run out on me, and I can't drive the damn thing myself. Rupp, I think you're a man who can see and not see, hear and not hear. Am I right?"

"Yes, sir," Bertie replied.

"Yes, I think so. Good, so you'll drive me up to the club this weekend. Now."

"But—but—" Bertie stammered. The big one cut him off with a wave of the hand.

"Relax, son, everything is provided. You'll get a change of clothes, it's like a costume party. You'll love it. _____ _____ spoke as he threw the keys at Bertie and climbed into the backseat. Bertie caught the keys mechanically and stood dumbly outside the car. "For chrissake, Rupp, get in."

Because he had trained himself to be like water and flow along the path of least resistance (or was it because little men were at work with jackhammers inside his cerebellum?), Bertie got in the car and sat down. The incriminating black box was in his trouser pocket. As he adjusted the rearview mirror before driving off, Bertie accidentally tilted it downward so he could see the backseat. Next to _____ _____ there was a stack of photocopies nearly four inches thick.

4

Big Boys Camp

_____ _____ dropped a set of directions onto the front seat and closed the partition; within minutes he appeared to be asleep.

Bertie glanced in the rearview mirror, then examined the directions. The destination, in the foothills of mountains some fifty miles from the coast, was marked with the cross formée, like one would see on pirate treasure maps in Hollywood movies.

Paved road ended several miles before their destination. Bertie, following instructions on the map, turned off the state highway onto an old logging road marked only by a crude sign with the three letters, BBC. Bertie assumed that the _C_ stood for Club, and he spent some moments speculating on the two _B_'s as the Rolls motored slowly through the underbrush. The road was a smooth one, not the set of humpbacked ruts one might have expected. Three and a half miles into the forest they passed under a crude archway with another hand-lettered sign:

CAMP TATHAGATA

Fifty yards later Bertie's hair stood on end as two armed guards stepped from behind trees and into his path.

Bertie braked to a stop, but after a quick look in the backseat the security men waved him on. Around the next corner he passed under a second archway, like the first a long board supported by two poles and childishly painted:

BIG BOYS CAMP

He pulled up behind a row of expensive cars, incongruous in the rustic setting. The letters *B*, *B*, and *C* cartwheeled across Bertie's mind's eye like the spinning newspapers of a thirties film montage.

The main camp building was an old timber lodge. An army tent was pitched next to the huge log cabin. A group of middle-aged and elderly men were gathered in the grassy clearing between the rows of cars and the lodge.

A playing field had been carved out of the forest, and there was a small man-made lake with a beachfront of imported sand. A gaggle of canoes bobbed beside a dock. The scene was made surreal by unobtrusive but ever-present security in the form of occasional passes by a helicopter, and by the clothing of the men. They were dressed like boys, in polo shirts and gym shorts. Nicknames from their childhoods were lettered on their chests: "Scooter," "Pee Wee," "Whizzer," "Sluggo." Bertie was stunned to recognize among the crowd of erstwhile youths two of the nine sitting justices of the Supreme Court.

An authoritative-looking man with a clipboard in his hand and a whistle around his neck motioned to Bertie from the tent entrance. "You can wait in here." Bertie was shown inside where cots had been set up, and drivers like him were lounging, reading, drinking sodas; it reminded Bertie of the waiting area of bus terminals. "Or you can come out and play."

"I'll play," said Bertie.

"What's your nickname?"

After a moment's thought Bertie said: "Gizmo."

The man wrote on his board. "Okay, Gizmo, here's your shorts and sneakers. Your shirt will be out in a minute. Dinner's at six. Right now is free time, do whatever you want, but don't leave the security perimeter.

Bertie wondered how they knew his clothing and shoe sizes. He hadn't seen _____ _____ since his arrival, so while he was waiting for his shirt he peeked out the tent entrance, but all the automobiles were gone, and _____ _____ was nowhere to be seen. Bertie's shirt arrived, still warm from the heat transfer process for the lettering.

"Have fun, son," said the man with the whistle and the clipboard. He patted Bertie on the head and sent him out into the front yard.

Bertie felt silly and self-conscious in his new outfit, but apparently no one else did. Groups of campers were engaged in childlike games on the playing field. Some of the canoes had been taken out, and there was a terrific water fight. Bertie noticed two similarities among the campers: They were all men of power, and all of them had that exaggerated tan that one gets under a sunlamp. He joined in as best he could, and later that afternoon he was amazed to find himself tied together in a three-legged race with the chairman of the board of one of the country's top ten corporations. This man had taken Killer as his nickname. He was a renowned collegiate football player in his day, and in the race he ran for glory with Bertie strapped to him and dangling helplessly a few inches off the ground. They won their first heat.

"Way to go, Gizmo," the burly executive muttered to Bertie under his breath. "Good strategy." He was as excited and intent as if he were closing a merger.

Dinner that evening was a weenie roast with toasted marshmallows. Bertie was a vegetarian, so the hot dogs were out, and puffed white sugar appealed even less to him than meat.

He ate the toasted buns and marveled that bread could be made so poorly and still taste good.

There was a mood of great anticipation. Bertie could distinguish this group from any bunch of seven-year-old boys only by the surreptitious drinking of alcohol from slim flasks.

When the overage campers had eaten their fill of hot dogs, they gathered close around the camp fire. Everyone but Bertie seemed to know what was coming next. From behind the big lodge came a procession of robed figures bearing candles and torches. As they approached the uncertain light of the camp fire, their peaked cowls and the quirky shadows made them seem monstrously tall. Four of the shapes carried a cage suspended on poles, which they bore on their shoulders. Within the cage was a fiery-eyed demon, the likes of which Bertie had never dreamed he would see. It looked like a monkey, with flat forehead; bright, steely eyes; a round head; hairy cheeks; and no chin. But it stood upright in the cage, and it was dressed in finer robes than those worn by the men who hoisted it, still caged, onto a giant stump above the camp fire.

The strange, fierce creature bared its teeth in a fearsome grin. It surveyed the assemblage with a pair of eyes that seemed to shoot beams of light out as it stared. Then Bertie nearly died of fright and shock; it spoke.

"Welcome to Camp Tathagata," it said. "You bold men, lusting men, seeing feeling smelling hearing tasting men. The cream of your crop, I daresay. Which of you will stand up to old Monkey?"

No one moved forward. Instead, everyone cringed and fell backward as the upright ape snarled and rattled the bars of its pen.

"Ah, just as I thought. Very well, it is time for your story. Put no more logs on the fire; let the embers burn down while I tell my tale."

"If you remember from the last telling, Tripitaka, Pigsy,

Sandy, and I, Sun Wu Kong, Great Monkey Sage, were swept up into Paradise. But life in Heaven grew dull for this restless, reckless ape. I gave a tug on the fabric at the outermost edge of the farthest extreme of the universe, and soon everything was rushing toward the core.

"In a few thousand years the sky was filled with encroaching suns and moons, and at last there remained only a mass of energy resting and glowing and shining in the Void. Thus was the Scripture fulfilled."

> All the differentiations of mountains and seas, rivers and forests blended into one another and faded away leaving only the flower-adorned unity of the Primal Cosmos, not dead and inert but alive with rhythmic life and light, vibrant with transcendental sounds of songs and rhymes, melodiously rising and falling and merging and then fading away into silence.*

"All that had been was not. All that was to be existed only in Potentiality. I clapped my hands in delight. Presently there was an explosion that defied all adjectives. I caused the starry heavens to be born. Swirling gasses coalesced and cooled into galaxies and suns and planets. The cycle of existence began again in the soupy broth of a warm ocean."

Bertie let out his breath with a gasp. A monkey was telling the creation story to American capitalists in the fantasy camp of their lost childhoods. Bertie was in dire danger of losing his perspective.

"I created them in my own image," the bizarre narrator continued. "In my own image. I gave them a land of milk

*Surangama Sutra, *A Buddhist Bible*, edited by Dwight Goddard.

and honey to play in, and I left their brains as empty as a polished mirror to the cloudless sky, as still and pure as a windless day. Oh, yes, I gave them the best of everything, and they could have gone on forever, playing and swaying in the branches and picking the lice off each other and living the life of ease. But they betrayed me."

"They came down from the trees and befouled the land with their filth. They made unnatural things and prized them more than the simple pleasures I had set for them. Worst of all, they began to think for themselves and forgot their original purpose, which was to *glorify me*."

With a guttural roar the ape threw itself against the door of its cage. Grown men screamed like little boys and fell over one another. The hooded bearers edged closer to the cage, but it was secure. The eloquent ape resumed its tirade.

"You! You betrayed me! Your doubt has weakened me. Your sins have defiled me. My power is gone. *Grrr!* But, fools, in your arrogance you will destroy yourselves. Yes, and you'll do it by imitating me. You think that you can create with machines that which I became a god to do. You don't know the power you are loosening on yourselves. Here is my prophecy: *You will all die! Yeech! Yeech!"* The monkey abruptly threw off its cap and robes, screaming in gibberish and racing around the confines of its cage. It had reverted completely to an animal state. Its keepers draped a heavy velour covering over it; the noise stopped instantly, and they carried the cage away. The camp leader reappeared from the shadows. He mounted the stump where the monkey had held forth.

"That's your scary horror story for tonight, campers. Let's all go to our tents now. There's cocoa and cookies for everybody, then it's lights out. We've got a big day planned for tomorrow."

Bertie had the feeling that everyone else understood the events of the evening, that he was the only one to whom the whole thing had been surreal, fantastic, incomprehensible.

Had he been watching a clever actor? Was it an animal trained to move its lips in sync with a recording? Why were these hardcore, conservative businessmen suddenly interested in spiritual matters such as the Book and the sayings of this monkey? Was it really their prisoner?

The other campers had gone off for their bedtime snack; they were already in their tents singing songs and carrying on the psychological charade of youthfulness. Bertie sat alone by the dying camp fire. A song drifted to him through the clear night air:

> . . . never is heard a discouraging word
> And the skies are not cloudy all day.

_____ _____ had disappeared at the beginning of the weekend. Bertie wondered where he'd gone. Why wasn't he with the others? Had he witnessed tonight's performance? Bertie's brain seethed with unanswered questions. He waited in his bunk until all the other campers were asleep; then, with newfound boldness born of the quest for the Book, he followed the path from the camp fire to the rear of the lodge. He had noticed that only camp leaders had entered the building.

One window was lit by the glow of candles from the earlier procession. Bertie crept up to it and peeked in by standing on a stack of firewood.

The cloth cover to the cage had been thrown back, and the ape crouched in one corner eating rice and vegetables from a bowl, using chopsticks to do so. Four men sat at a table in the austere room, which retained the sparse character of a hunting lodge. One of the four was _____ _____. The other three were men of equal prominence. On the table was the set of precious photocopies, divided into piles and spread out before the seated men. They studied the pages like scholars or cryptographers, and from what little conversation Bertie could hear, he deduced that they believed the Book to be in code. What hidden meaning they searched for, Bertie dared not guess.

Once _____ _____ got up and walked over to the cage.

"You could tell us, you son of a bitch." The grotesque fear and anger in _____ _____'s voice made Bertie shiver. The monkey stared dolefully at _____ _____ and said nothing.

Very late in the evening the candles guttered out. Bertie had fallen asleep, head resting on the window ledge, a moment before after two hours of strenuous watchfulness. The scraping of a chair when the men left the room awakened him. He rubbed his eyes and pinched himself, and with blurry vision he peered into the darkened room. There was no glass, only a screen window that couldn't be opened from the outside.

Bertie could feel the ape's gaze, and those eyes glowed like a cat's in the fuzzy darkness and seemed to grow brighter when Bertie addressed him. "Mr. Monkey," Bertie whispered. "Pssst. Hey, Monkey." Bertie balanced precariously on the cut logs propped against the side of the house. "Come on," Bertie pleaded. "I know you can talk. We—we believe the same things. I'm not one of them."

The monkey looked at him balefully. Suddenly a beam of light shot out from its eyes and held Bertie transfixed. The ray disappeared—at the speed of light—and Bertie was released. Now the ape spoke to him. "Yes, disciple, I recognize you. Poor fellow, prepare for much sadness in your life. There is one you should see."

"I want to take you out of here." Bertie groaned with urgency, but he was interrupted.

"No. My time is finished. I'm dead already; what you see

is mere habit-energy. But there is one who can help you. See him."

"Who? Who is he?" Bertie begged for an answer.

"He's in the Bronx Zoo. A relative of mine. And yours, too, if you stop to think of it. He's—"

Just then the stack of wood gave way and tumbled Bertie to the ground. Lights went on in the lodge. Armed men rushed out of the front door, but Bertie had already scrambled down the path to the tents. He tiptoed into his assigned place, careful not to wake two sleeping companions, and slipped fully dressed into his sleeping bag.

The second day began with a pancake and Ovaltine breakfast and proceeded through archery and trail lore to a late-afternoon powwow at which they all dressed like Indians, sat cross-legged in a circle, and smoked the pipe of peace. Bertie hoped and prayed for a second appearance of the monkey, but it was not to be. They were sent to the showers to wash off their war paint and emerged, miraculously transformed back into the same worldly, important men who had arrived on Friday afternoon.

Bertie didn't see _____ _____ all day, but when Bertie came out of the dressing room in his office clothes (which had been cleaned and pressed in the interim), _____ _____ was waiting for him in the car, which had conveniently reappeared.

"Take me to the airport, Rupp. Catch any?"

"Huh?" said Bertie.

"I don't know where you were, Rupp, but I was out on the lake fishing for bass."

Bertie went home and started packing for his trip to New York.

5

Eva in Inner Space

Zooming along at six hundred miles an hour, Bertie looked down on the geometrically arranged Midwest of his youth. Somewhere down there were millions and millions of tons of corn. That knowledge made him feel temporarily secure, though unlike most blasé travelers, Bertie never lost the awful sensation of tremendous speed when riding in a jet.

He had used the sum total of a modest bank account and had given notice on his apartment so as not to pay rent. On the word of a monkey he was flying across the continent to an uncertain future.

The stewardess came by with an air-sealed plastic pouch of peanuts and an air-sealed plastic pouch of red wine for Bertie. A plane ride like this was a special treat for the former mathematical wizard. He knew that computers, not men, had designed the sleek machine, and that a computer, not a man, controlled its movement at this moment. Sometimes it seemed like the most natural thing in the world. Other times, he was awestruck by it: He and a few dozen others in two or three laboratories in the late 1950s had set the patterns and parameters for the existences of untold millions of humans.

Life looks neat and orderly from thirty thousand feet in
an electronic flying machine. When one comes back down
to earth, the contrast can be jarring, especially if one lands
in New York City. Bertie had been there a few times for
conferences in his earlier incarnation as an IBM man. Nothing
had prepared him for the shocking deterioration of the place
since he had last visited.

Because he had very little money, Bertie took a bus to the
A train into the city instead of a taxicab. The train was a
rolling mural done in a Day-Glo spray-paint medium. Like
the canvas of a poor artist, the walls of the train had developed
a patina from reuse. Perhaps a dozen previous layers, each
imperfectly steam-cleaned, gave depth and subtlety to the
most recent efforts. The inside of each car was done in the
same motif—seats, windows, doors, and all. Bertie saw in
the paintings an expression of some great repressed energy.

The train set off in an agony of screeching from unoiled
moving parts. Gentle Bertie could not have looked more
vulnerable if he had hung a sign around his neck that read:
TOURIST. Some guardian angel must have watched over him,
because he managed to arrive at his destination without being
robbed.

Bertie had made arrangements for an old friend to put him
up, another IBM dropout with whom Bertie maintained a
fitful correspondence. Roscoe lived in New York's Hell's
Kitchen, so Bertie was able to walk from the train station to
his apartment.

Bertie found the building and pressed the appropriate button next to his friend's name. The door made a clicking sound,
and Bertie pushed it open. He puffed his way up five flights
of stairs until he found the right number, then he pushed
another button. A tiny peephole slid open, and through it
Bertie could see an eyeball staring at him. Next came the
sound of several sets of locks being turned. At last the door
opened, and there was Roscoe Hankins, dressed entirely in

black: black Converse All-Stars, black socks, black jeans, black shirt, and shoulder-length black hair.

"Hello, Bertram." Roscoe extended a milk-white hand, but his grip was firm.

"How was your trip?"

"The first three thousand miles were great. The last fifteen were scary."

"You ain't seen nothin' yet, brother. You said something on the phone about going to the Bronx."

"The zoo."

"This whole town is one big zoo. Ride through the Bronx tomorrow and you'll know what I mean. But come in, come in."

The two old friends spent the evening getting reacquainted. Roscoe seemed to be living in slightly accelerated fast motion. Every movement was speeded up. He drank countless cups of coffee through the night and smoked cigarettes one after the other, lighting the next with the butt of the previous one.

"I'm a pantomime artist, Bertram. I work the streets, you know, do the movie lines and Washington Square, benefits, birthday parties, crazy telegrams, you name it. Commercials, films, anything. Amazingly, I make a living. Not many performers can say that.

"Saturday is the big antiwar demonstration at the UN. I'm working on a special piece for it. We hope to have half the city there."

Bertie was excited by the idea of many people protesting the thing that had obsessed him for years. He hoped it was not too late. Lately the leaders of the two great powers had become increasingly strident and warlike in their statements. Both sides had just brought on line several new weapons systems, including particle-beam guns, mounted on satellites, that could shoot down missiles as they left the atmosphere on their intercontinental journeys of destruction.

Bertie discovered that Roscoe's pale skin, his late-night

hours, and his unhealthy physical habits were not unique; they were endemic to most New Yorkers. Roscoe rarely saw the sun, except as it rose while he crawled, like a creature of the night, toward his windowless bedroom.

On the train to the zoo the next morning Bertie passed through an area where it seemed the war had already started. Only a battle could have caused the kind of devastation Bertie witnessed from the East White Plains express, an ancient and defaced vehicle traversing the South Bronx on creaking trestles. Beneath was a grim landscape that reminded Bertie of pictures of Dresden. Many buildings were reduced to rubble. Others stood as charred shells or as fragile, picturesque ruins, while the sturdiest and most complete were inhabited by the fiercely haggard denizens of this urban miasma.

The zoo was a surprising patch of green in the relentless grayness of the Bronx. Bertie bought a ticket and entered the animal prison, a place he normally feared and shunned as an example of man's inhumanity to Nature. He went to the monkey house.

The primates were kept in a long, low building made up of two rows of cages. Tourists from all over the world strolled through the wide walkway. Each cage was labeled with the Latin names for the animal within. Often several genera were mingled together.

Incidents between humans and zoo animals had increased markedly. Three weeks previous, a man had been mauled to death by a polar bear. In the past week a female gorilla had snatched a baby from its mother, but instead of killing it the ape had nursed the infant at her breast until zookeepers were able to subdue her with tranquilizer darts. Most disturbing of all, animals both here in the zoo and also out in the free world were exhibiting signs of psychological stress, as before an earthquake or other natural disaster. The small herds of deer stampeded senselessly in their pens. Hibernating animals entered their lairs though it was late summer and well before their dormant season. Out at sea, dolphins and whales were beaching themselves with suicidal fury and in frightening numbers, as if they had resolved en masse that the future was too grim to face.

In this dismal setting Bertie wandered with a bag of peanuts in one hand and a mustard-covered pretzel in the other. He asked the gibbons, the lemurs, the marmosets, the ringtails, and the spider monkeys, but none in the ape house would respond to him.

The air was heavy with the smell of baboon shit as Bertie walked along the line of bars and examined the faces behind them. Some of them seemed wise, with softly tufted, wispy gray beards like those Oriental sages might wear. Some screeched and scratched and mindlessly masturbated.

"Hello," said Bertie to a particularly dignified-looking orangutan with deep-set, motionless eyes and a flaming orange crown. The ape stared back at him silently. Perhaps it was some other animal that Monkey had meant when he sent Bertie across the continent. Bertie was sure he had heard him say the Bronx Zoo. No matter what the effort involved, Bertie was determined to find the one he sought. He ignored the amused and disdainful glances of others, and he didn't react when two cruel teenage girls sang "Talk to the Animals" and laughed in his face.

He tried the bird house, but the cold, transparent eyes of the aviary's inhabitants were rigid and unwavering in their gazes and did not communicate with him.

"Do you know Monkey?" he asked the hippopotamus, but it only grunted and yawned and slid backward into its pool. Bertie tried purring to the great cats. He howled at the wolves' den, and when he came to the hyenas' cage, he mimicked them loudly.

"Where are you, Wise One?" Bertie implored the animals in the zoo, but though they talked to each other, none of them would give Bertie the time of day.

Almost in a panic now because the thought of failure was too dreadful to conceive, Bertie flitted from cage to cage, screaming, "Great Monkey Sage has sent me, come out, come out!" until two men came up behind him, and one of them stuck him with an electric prod, and suddenly the wind went out of him the mad wind worlded him mad world winded him a protoplasmic blast oh the blastic transcendental qualities light more light more light he cried. Waving arms like seaweed in the tide more light he cried synapses collapsing around him like cards on a table like birds of a furry feather together.

Pant he pants he panted *ahhhgggghhh* they stuffed his mouth with an ether cheesecloth suppose he was unconscious when it happened no not the swoon he was swooning now but the real thing oh God spirit suffocated under the dense drug fog he clawed out at faces pressing down on him like noses on glass.

Swimming upside down in his own head Bertie blanked out Bertie blew out Bertie bounced out and in and out and in and sometimes he saw with perfect clarity the corner of a door or hair on an arm or the scratches on the window how they sliced the light in planes so pure crystal rays of it shooting out to heaven above below to the left of him to the right of him.

He was in a vehicle now and moving down a street, but where and why and when he forgot again as the round spun in, exploded.

Oh Bertie hero traveler, Arabian knight, Odysseus of the nuclear age, how he fell. He thought the world could not be so deep as he fell in fearful descent. No weight held him now, no gravity applied. He cartwheeled through space, while down below he could see himself stretched out in an ambulance.

6

The Buffalo Roam

One day Bertie lay floating above the cot in his room at Bellevue, his mind and body, like sun and moon, rotating freely yet attached by invisible bonds. This freewheeling state of grace was so perfect for meditation, Bertie let his mind wander; it ended up in Plains, Kansas, where it saw an event witnessed that evening by millions on the network news broadcast.

A state highway ran through the middle of Plains in classic Midwestern fashion. Plains hummed and bustled its way toward oblivion like most American cities. An ICBM installation just outside of town made it particularly vulnerable to visitation, but its citizens continued to buy cars and have affairs and get drunk at Grange meetings, although there had been a recent drop-off in applications for thirty-year mortgages.

The first person to see them was Phil Hays, the radio announcer at WPLN, whose cinder-block one-room studio stood next to the broadcast antenna three miles north of town. He was outside stretching his legs while a recorded cassette played four minutes and seventeen seconds of advertisements when he noticed a black cloud of dust moving down the broad valley out of the north. He stared at it while his mind tried to create some context for it. He watched it for a minute more, saw that it was something huge and awesome, but instead of becoming afraid, Phil Hays saw a chance for a moment of personal glory. He was about to be hit by a very big news story. Whatever it was, it was his scoop.

For the next seven minutes and twelve seconds, or until he was trampled to death by a stampeding herd that demolished the studio, the antenna, and Phil Hays all in an instant, he did his best impression of Joseph Cotton in *War of the Worlds*.

"... We interrupt these regularly scheduled announcements for this incredible bulletin. Folks! People! It's me, Phil. I'm up at the studio! There's something coming from the north, I can't tell what it is yet. Might be a tornado! Everybody should get to cover! Can you hear it? I'm going back outside with the binoculars to see what I can see. I'll leave the mike open. This is Phil Hays live from WPLN, three miles north of Plains, Kansas."

The microphone broadcast a low rumble like approaching thunderheads, punctuated by the slapping of the screen door, twice.

"I'm back. It's definitely not weather. It's on the ground, whatever it is. All right, now. Easy, Phil. Can you feel it? The earth is shaking under me. I'm going to take a minute here and run a long cord out the door so I can broadcast and watch at the same time. Just a moment."

Everybody in town listened to Phil in the morning. Down at the barbershop they were cracking up and saying what a card that Phil was. Somebody mentioned his Crazy-Tie contest, and somebody else brought up the Daffy Easter Duck Egg Hunt.

"Okay, I'm outside now. Goddamn. Dogdamn. I can't believe it. It's coming right straight down Highway 35, but wider, maybe half a mile wide, raising up so much dust that it's getting dark. It must be out by Charley Smith's place about now."

Phil wasn't far wrong. Charley Smith's place wasn't there anymore.

"Got to be a herd of cattle, or maybe a whole bunch of crazies on motorcycles, or dune buggies. Hold on!"

Phil laid the microphone on the ground where it picked up the aural and physical vibrations of the approaching danger. The intrepid—and doomed—announcer ran up a few yards and peered into his binoculars. At this distance, through the excellent Bausch and Lomb's he had pirated out of the Air Force, Phil was able to see the massive shoulders of the charging lead buffalo, even their flaring nostrils and inflamed eyes. It took several seconds for him to realize what he was seeing. He sprinted back to the microphone.

"It's buffalo! Forty, fifty, no—maybe a hundred thousand of them! The biggest herd I've ever seen. I didn't think there were this many buffalo left on earth. Where have they come from? Oh, boy, this is exciting! Get inside, everybody! It's going to be like the running of the bulls, only wilder, a thousand times. They're getting close now, maybe half a mile. The noise is tremendous, the hooves and the bellowing. I can't see any end to them, the dust is so thick. I've got to get back inside. I could run for it in the truck, but I'm going to stay right here. They'll go around the building."

He was wrong. Nine minutes later they reached town. Instead of channeling themselves into the streets of Plains, the buffalo threw themselves into walls, crashed through plate-glass windows, leveled buildings with the force of numbers. They overran the town; they tore down the gleaming white granaries, not to feed but because they were in the path of the herd. They hurled themselves against the stronger structures until there were mountains of dead beasts piled up; and still more came, trampling on the bodies of their kind, until

by sheer weight they toppled every obstacle. Not one person
in the town survived.

The attack lasted fifteen minutes; when it was over, Plains
was gone. The prairie wind blew over the flatness.

The area was littered with mutilated buffalo, exhausted,
dying animals. The survivors thundered out of the south end
of what used to be a town and were slaughtered by helicopter
gunships in a carnage that might have offended even Buffalo
Bill.

7

Missile Fields

Bertie knew that the target of the buffalo was the missile site at the southern edge of town. The creatures miscalculated how long it would take them to rumble through Plains. They died violently and uselessly at the base gate, in the frenzied stench of napalm.

Beneath this scene, far below the deepest roots of a field of Bertie's beloved corn, was a cave carved out of the primeval schist. The air inside the cave was temperature-controlled and humidity-regulated. The light sources were selected on the basis of experiments that demonstrated their positive effects on the alertness of the subjects. The drinking water was purified, the food sterilized.

Space Cadet Reggie Wilson, Starblaster, was on duty. The Air Force thought he was Sergeant Reginald Wilson, expert in launch systems, one of a two-man team required to fire the cylinder of liquid explosives sitting outside the cave door. Recently a funny thing had happened to Sergeant Wilson. Cleaning fluid spilled in the ventilating system had seeped out the grate next to Sergeant Wilson's desk, odorless but mind-boggling. Reginald hadn't been the same since. In fact, though he told no one, he now believed he was a Starblaster and had reprogrammed his babies from the shipyards at Murmansk to a different target. In a few weeks Reggie would start World War III.

If a hundred thousand buffalo couldn't stop him, who could? Reggie thought as he gazed dreamily at a waveform readout of the machine's present state of readiness. Just as Army intelligence and the CIA would later assume that the Russians were somehow controlling the buffalo, Reggie thought they were sent by some galactic villain.

Carl Renstrom, the other member of the launch crew, might have been mistaken for a younger Bertie. He'd just finished recircuiting a terminal screen to play the complicated video game Planet Smasher. Reggie thought starmen were attacking him with buffalo. Carl wasted his brilliance mastering toy simulations of war. Together they presided over the firing sequence of ten multimegaton warheads atop the single rocket buried beside them.

The two of them rarely spoke; there was little need, and even before Reggie's recent psychochemical transformation, they had talked across oceans of cultural estrangement. Reggie did a thousand sit-ups a day in the bunker and preened his Afro. Carl smoked, had bad skin, and ate junk food. They solved the problem of coexistence through the use of individual stereo headphones.

Tonight the first glimmerings of a crisis manifested themselves. Carl real aloud from a scientific article about nuclear weapons. "In all the known universe, temperatures of equal heat are found only in such transient phenomena as exploding supernovae. . . . The explosion begins as a shock wave, traveling inward in a shrinking concentric sphere, gaining in force and temperature as it proceeds."*

When Reggie heard these words, it occurred to him that

The Fate of the Earth, Jonathan Schell.

Carl Renstrom might be an alien. *Renstrom*, he thought. *What kind of weird name was that? Always playing around with the computer shit. Good thing he don't know nothin' about targeting and stays with propulsion, or he'd figure out what I done.* And so the seed was sown for a monstrous growth to rise out of the Kansas earth, blossoming flowers of evil.

"Hey, dude, turn that thing down." Reggie glared at his nemesis. From the other side of the room came the relentless violence of synthesized explosions.

8

SPOM Meets SPOOS

About this time Bertie was sinking toward his fragile life-support system and preparing for reentry into reality. They had drugged him. They had interrogated him. They had probed into the small, meaningful recesses of his soul, those hidden hills and valleys of experience that, taken together, constitute the geography of a personality. All the while Bertie had hovered above and watched the proceedings with detached interest, or he had floated off to Kansas and other places.

Finally they had to let him go. The hospitals were overrun with cases far worse than Bertie's, people whose symptoms of nucleomitophobia had progressed into radical psychoses. Sometimes, as in the animal world, this dementia occurred in groups.

Bertie's friend Roscoe belonged to such a group: The Society for the Preservation of Mankind. They believed that man was an endangered species. On the day Bertie was released from Bellevue, Roscoe took him to a meeting of SPOM.

They walked together up the West Side to Fifty-ninth Street, then across the southern end of the park. Bertie's legs were shaky from weeks of inactivity, but his vision was clear.

The point of the gathering that evening was to find new forms of protest. Only a week previous, a man had scaled the fence surrounding an old Titan missile and poured Holy Water on the nose cone. (There were those, even among the military, who believed that the leaky, obsolete Titans were a greater danger to their possessors than to the enemy.) Many SPOM members were charismatic Catholics who were sure that a dose of Aqua Sacrae would neutralize bombs.

Mrs. Bremens owned the lavish Central Park South condo where the meeting was held. In bold purple on a white porcelain-steel easel she wrote names of great protesters from the past: Thoreau, Gandhi, Martin Luther King, Jr. She listed current dramatic and successful protests, including the Holy Water incident, the pouring of blood on files and military machinery by the Berrigan brothers, and European street protests where the participants dressed in the forms of specters, skeletons, golems, schmürzs, and other archetypal images of death.

Bertie slumped on an ottoman at the back of the room and observed the woman's energetic command. Her zeal and devotion to the cause were unquestionable. She had gathered a crowd of liberal West Siders to her home, and now she fueled them with a history lesson on protest. The group was young, forceful, successful. Mrs. Bremens's apartment was elegant, valuable, and triple-insured. Contradictions seesawed through his head.

"What we need now," Mrs. Bremens was saying, "is some new forms of protest that will make everyone perk up and listen. Are there any ideas? Please speak up."

She had moved the dining room table out and arranged all the chairs in rows. Why, she wondered, did it feel like a party instead of a meeting? Maybe it was the buffet. Next time, she decided, no open bar, no buffet, and right to business from the start.

"How about if we all dress up as extinct animals?" a man asked.

"Sure, Ralph, you can be the dodo," suggested his wife. Everyone laughed. However, the idea did start a discussion. The strange episode of the buffalo in Kansas and other vivid demonstrations that nature was in the midst of some little understood trauma were mentioned. Bertie could have told them the connection between these events and the future, but he sat silently and tugged the black cap Roscoe had given him farther down over the bristly hairs of his recently shaved head.

"We need something big and splashy. We've got to have media coverage." The speaker was a news reporter for a cable television station. His incongruously tanned skin made Bertie think of Big Boys Camp. No one had any big, splashy suggestions.

Then a peculiar, hypnotic voice broke the silence. "We could kill ourselves. Remember the Vietnamese monks?"

Bertie's head snapped up.

"Who are you?" Mrs. Bremens suddenly asked. "I don't believe I know you. Are you a friend of someone here?"

"We are all friends." The speaker stepped forward, a smallish man, dark-skinned, with close-cropped hair and brown eyes. "I bring you greetings from another organization, one which, like yours, is dedicated to the salvation of species."

"What group is that?"

"My card."

Mrs. Bremens accepted a small block of lucite and read aloud the words engraved there: "Vith Pankas, Society for the Preservation of Outer Space. SPOOS."

People started to laugh; one aggressive New Yorker scoffed: "Ridiculous. Space isn't threatened, only the Earth."

"To think that," Vith spoke in a soothing yet firm tone, like a teacher addressing a favored pupil, "is to limit your sights to your immediate environment. Look up! Look out! You, your sun and moon, and the other eight planets, are substantially isolated from the nearest inhabited star system. You float in a little cluster in the void, yet who knows what future may be lost if people extinguish themselves now? Perhaps your destiny is in the stars."

"Inhabited?" Mrs. Bremens gasped.

"I beg your pardon?" Vith replied.

"You said . . ."

"What—do any of you not believe that there is life on other worlds?" Vith made a noise something like a high-pitched squeal and a rapid series of clicks. Everybody stepped back from him. He reached under his peculiar seamless and pocketless brown coat. The group withdrew farther from him, but he produced an innocuous-looking notebook covered with the same fabric as his coat. In fact, Bertie noticed, all of his clothing was made of this drab, featureless material: his shirts, his socks, even his shoes. Vith Pankas was monochromatic.

On the face of the notebook was the only flash of color: a six-letter word in bright gold relief. At a glance it appeared to be ordinary embossing. Then Bertie saw two things simultaneously. He was sure it was simultaneously, even though he believed that the mind could not hold two thoughts at once. He saw that the letters were moving, not across the surface but within themselves; the gold was bubbling and swirling without changing the elegant shapes, and while he realized this, he had his second revelation. The letters were an acronym for the Book: *TABOTD*.

This was confirmed when Vith spoke.

"Listen to a passage from a section of *TABOTD*"—he pronounced it as a two-syllable word; the effect was like a dolphin speaking Tibetan—"known also as the Book of Warnings. Here are a few for you to contemplate:

CHARLATANS MAY BE TAKEN FOR SAGES.
A SECOND OF CARELESSNESS, A LIFETIME OF
REGRET.
A LIFETIME OF CARELESSNESS, A SECOND OF
REGRET.
SOME RESTRICTIONS APPLY.
NO CHILDREN, NO PETS.
THE SURVIVORS WILL ENVY THE DEAD.

"What did I just say, Bertie?"

"The survivors will envy the dead." Vith and Bertie gazed at each other across a void wider than Bertie ever could have imagined.

"Now I'm going to tell you about your world. What you learn tonight may not help you to save it, but at least you will enter eternity less ignorant."

The room was awash with noiselessly echoing shadows. Vith had hypnotized the group. No one moved or spoke. When Vith resumed speaking, he addressed Bertie alone.

"Yes, young man, many of the things you feared, hoped, and suspected are true. First, there is a bird in the jungles of Brazil whose call is a vestigial remnant of my own language. Your world was visited at least once previously. This helps explain why your race plodded along for a million years and flourished in the past six thousand. Secondly—and this is very important—for every object there is a sound, not necessarily a word, which is its exact resonant vibratory equivalent. Chinese language, which dispenses with prepositions, conjunctions, and modifiers, comes closest to this principle, so it is not surprising that they are the people who have come nearest to understanding the transcendental forces of the cosmos.

"As I was saying, the survivors will envy the dead."

With these words he recalled the group from its collective trance. Like most hypnosis subjects, the members had no recall of their altered state.

"You have only your voices with which to protest. To do anything more is to become like those you fear. In fact," Vith said with a smile, "the best and most effective action would be for everyone to do nothing, but as a people, you don't have the discipline for it."

"What, a general strike?" someone asked.

"Yes," Vith answered in a tone that made Bertie think of his high-school civics teacher. "Those who would destroy each other in the name of political systems are greedy, lustful men. Their power depends on the cooperation of many people. If you deny them your energy, they are powerless."

Somewhere in Bertie's memory banks, his sophisticated, internal word processor was comparing the content, linguistic style, and delivery of Vith Pankas with earlier tapes on file and preparing to issue an analysis to his present consciousness, but before this could happen, Vith disappeared. Though no one wanted to talk about it afterward, the consensus was that he had vanished "into thin air" after catching everybody with the old dodge, "Oh, look up there," while pointing to the ceiling. Everybody looked, and when they looked back, he was gone.

The rest of the evening was spent in a spiritless debate of the alternatives. A sense of hopelessness pervaded the affair. Vith had pointed the way for them, but by doing so he had also made them see how far they had to go. Outside of small gatherings like these, sentiment in Bertie's country had not turned against nuclear weapons. In the other dangerous country of power, no protest was allowed. There public sentiment took the form of staggering increases in the consumption of vodka.

9

Attack of the Slot Machine Zombies

Bertie's trip to New York, from the Bronx Zoo to Bellevue, had been a disaster. Vith had shown him that the great uprising of protest against the inevitable, Bertie's last hope, would never come about. The crisis had arrived too soon. Too many people still clung to old-fashioned notions of patriotism, glory, victory. The rest were numb. Yet, despite these setbacks, a change had occurred in Bertie. Certainty had replaced doubt in his mind, and with certitude came fortitude. There was a new edge in his voice, a decisiveness that, in its early stages appeared as rude boisterousness.

With less than a hundred dollars in his pocket, Bertie could not afford to fly back to California. He walked from Roscoe's to Port Authority Bus Terminal, a kind of mecca for the Berties of the world. For seventy-five dollars he was able to buy a ticket that entitled him to a two-week tour of bus stations, in many Eastern, Midwestern and Far Western cities. Roscoe had packed him a small hamper full of vegetarian food, but Bertie found himself spending time in the terminal cafés drinking coffee from Styrofoam cups at dawn, sneaking around the corner from the station to smoke precious pinches from his hoard of New York White sewer-grown marijuana.

While Bertie traveled, events were occurring that accelerated the pace of the now inevitable conflict between the superpowers. Mistrust and suspicion could not be maintained for such a long time without a release of the accumulated pressure. The focal point of the latest incident was not the Mideast, as both Biblical fanatics and CIA intelligence experts predicted, but rather an obscure corner of the world, an island in the South Pacific whose chief export was guano, bird shit, and an inferior grade of shit, at that. A presidential plan, leaked to the press, called for evacuation of major cities if the situation intensified. Instead of reassuring the public, the plan caused a panic. It called for a period of three days, during which both sides would evacuate their populations from urban centers to the countryside, after which war could begin. The idea that such an event could be planned in advance was repugnant to many people. Huge new protests occurred, but there were other effects. Many people quit their jobs. Resort areas were jammed with people out for a last fling. Crime and drug abuse rose to unprecedented levels.

The bus carrying Bertie rolled across the Arizona desert, halting at the old stagecoach stops: Williams, Kingman, Peach Springs. As it approached Las Vegas the bus grew crowded with anxious people hurrying to get there in time to lose all their money before the world ended.

The government decided not to discourage this kind of activity, since the evacuation had not yet been ordered. Indeed, it was merely a plan, although the very fact that it existed signaled the desperation and fanaticism of the time. The mood on the bus was festive in the way a condemned man's last meal might be. The search for pleasure was fast and fierce.

Surreptitious drinking began several hours before the bus arrived in the terminal. When the door finally swung open in downtown Las Vegas, forty drunk and wild riders staggered off the bus to join the surging mobs in the streets. The scene was like New Orleans's Mardi Gras or Rio's Carnevale. Casino owners liked to keep the business in the clubs, with seventy-nine-cent double well drinks and dollar breakfasts where one could play keno while one ate, but the immense crowds had overflowed into the streets, and under the chaotic play of flashing marquee bulbs a mass of people danced and drank and reveled.

Bertie and the driver were the last two off the bus. The driver was irritated because he and Bertie were the only two sober people on the bus, and it bothered him that while he had to abstain, Bertie did so by choice.

"Here, pal, it's all yours." The driver chucked a set of keys at Bertie and, as an afterthought, placed his large cap on Bertie's smallish head. Then he turned and plunged into the crowd.

It was four o'clock in the morning. The terminal was as near closed as any place could be in the twenty-four-hour glow of Las Vegas. The bus line's offices were locked. The only activity was the ceaseless mechanical whir and jingle of slot machines placed by the departure gates. Here and everywhere else Bertie went that evening—including restaurants, hotel lobbies, gas stations, drugstores, and men's rooms—people were engaged in relentless battle with these machines.

Sensing the mood of the public, the casino owners had programmed their devices to pay off at a much lower percentage than usual. No one seemed to mind. They were there to lose it all.

Every big-name entertainer wanted to play the Strip for one last, desperate fling. This increased the gaily fatalistic atmosphere and swelled the numbers of those attracted to it. Bertie wandered, swept along by racing mobs stampeding from one club to the next. Stories of big losers circulated, extravagant tales of homes, land, whole companies wagered away.

At six-thirty Bertie had breakfast: three eggs, half a dozen dollar pancakes, potatoes, and coffee for ninety-nine cents. The server brought the skirt steak Bertie didn't want and wouldn't eat, because the cook couldn't believe anyone would order the breakfast special without it.

At eight o'clock Bertie pushed his way through milling celebrants to the terminal. The loading area was jammed with empty buses. Bertie's driver had not been the only one to defect. Bertie saw a driver being led to his bus by two armed guards who boarded the vehicle with him. Bertie was just about to approach the vacant window with his ticket when he remembered the cap on his head. In a panic he snatched it off, but unfortunately for Bertie, he had already been spotted by a distraught, overworked bus dispatcher in critical need of drivers.

Taking refuge in a phone booth, Bertie eluded a guard sent by the harried dispatcher. While hiding there Bertie called Roscoe in New York, wondering how people were reacting there.

"Bert, oh, my God, Bert, am I glad to hear from you! Where are you? Did they get you yet?"

"No, I ducked into this booth, but how did you know?"

"Bert, listen, the authorities are after you. Last week one of the monkeys in the zoo started talking—talking, Bert, you hear me? And it asked for you! What *were* you doing out there? You never told me."

It was true that Bertie had hidden the purpose of his visit to New York even from Roscoe, who had become his closest friend. He had made light of his psychotic episode, ascribing it to exhaustion and an overreaction by the Bellevue staff.

"The newspapers ran a little blurb: 'Anyone knowing the whereabouts of Bertram Rupp,' etcetera. I saw it in the *Post*. You know how I feel about dealing with the police, Bert, but

I thought you might be in trouble, had another spell, so I went to them. Boy, did they put me through it, especially when they found out about the antinuclear thing. An ape that talks, Bert? What's going on?"

Bertie told Roscoe about the night at Big Boys Camp but not about the episode with Vith Pankas; since Roscoe had been among those hypnotized, it might cause hard feelings.

"What should I do, Roscoe?" Bertie asked plaintively.

"This monkey needs your help, Bert. It refuses to talk with anyone but you. So far they haven't tortured it, but I wouldn't be surprised if they did. Come back, Bert. But don't come to my house. There's two guys downstairs in the lobby all the time. They follow me everywhere I go."

Nearly in tears, Bertie peeked over the top of the panel that formed his phone cubicle. No one was watching him. Without replying for a moment, Bertie held the phone in his hand and absentmindedly examined the confines of the space he occupied. Someone had scribbled graffiti on one wall: "Buy War Bonds."

"Roscoe . . . Roscoe, are you there?" Bertie suddenly yelled in the phone mouthpiece.

"Are *you* there is a better question."

"I am, I am."

"What are you going to do?"

"I'm coming back. Can you contact, uh, it for me?"

"I don't think so. It's not in its cage anymore, they've taken it somewhere. And don't call me at home again. I use pay phones these days."

When Bertie hung up, he had no idea how he was going to get back to the East Coast. He had little money. He had a bus ticket, but there were no drivers. After a few minutes of aimless walking among the crazed carousers, Bertie knew what he had to do. For the first time since he was six years old, when he had taken a box of Jujubes from Desjardin's Superette, Bertie became a thief. Bertie, the devout Buddhist, stole a bus.

10

Leave the Driving
to Bertie

It was easy. First he bought a newspaper. Then he threw away all but the classified ads, which he stuffed into the lining of the bus driver's cap until it almost fit his head. When this preparation was complete, he put on the hat and walked into the terminal where he was immediately seized by a uniformed guard, who brought him to the weary, bleary-eyed dispatcher.

"Another skunk, huh? You guys have shortened my life by fifteen years, you know that? Where's the pride in a job well done, the old company loyalty? Huh?" The poor fellow was coming undone, destroyed by the pressures of his work. Secretly he longed to rip off his clothes and join the party, but he was an Army man, the son and grandson of Army men, and this heritage kept him at his post.

"I'm going to send you so far away from here, you'll never get back. For you the party's over, understand? I want you to take this bus and drive east with it. This is a deadhead run to the St. Louis garage, got me? Huh? No passengers, no one is leaving, or if they are, they can't pay for it. Rufus here'll accompany you. I don't want to see you back here, understand?"

"Yes, sir!" Bertie replied, wondering all the while if he could figure out how to start the bus. On his trip West he had often sat in the front seat; he thought he could remember the location of the significant controls, including the switch inside the tiny driver's-side window that opened the door. But backing up would be a bigger problem.

Rufus was a very large, very black man whose ancestors were Nigerian chieftains. His skin was a burnished blue-black hue like carbon steel. He eyed Bertie with a blend of suspicion and contempt, flavored with a dollop of fear. Rufus felt about bus travel the way an ochlophobic would view the melee in the streets. He disliked everything about buses, starting with the nausea-producing diesel fumes that collected in great quantities inside the terminal. When Rufus was a chubby ten-year-old boy with the nickname Roof Ass, he got stuck in the cramped bathroom cubicle of an old humpbacked monster. The laughing driver stopped the bus to pry open the door and let him out. The humiliation and discomfort of that experience had left him with a permanent revulsion for buses and bus drivers. When he read in the Las Vegas paper that the bus company needed guards to escort drivers out of town, he jumped at the chance to recreate the scene of his youth in reverse.

"Yo, you, in de bus."

Bertie meekly complied. As soon as Bertie sat down, he quickly located the electric device that raised and lowered the seat. He set it at its highest position, then had to lower it a few inches so that his feet could reach the pedals. If Bertie squinted, he could view the road between the top rim of the steering wheel and the dashboard. Rufus watched these adjustments with concern.

"You sho' you a bus driver? Hain't they gots no height 'quirements?"

Bertie ignored him though his heart palpitated. Rufus looked back doubtfully at the dispatcher, who was pulling the hairs out of his head one by one and lining them up on his clipboard. Four of his buses had turned up outside of Reno in a trailer-park whorehouse. People were living in them.

The engine roared to life as soon as Bertie pressed the electronic ignition. Rufus sat down in the front seat across the aisle and clutched both armrests.

"Now, you drive good now, hear?"

"Relax, Rufus," Bertie said. He'd heard the dispatcher call the man by name. "Leave the driving to Bertie."

"Till we gets to St. Louis, you mah pris'ner."

With some effort, and not without taking a chunk out of the dispatcher's office, Bertie was able to back the bus into the street. Traffic moved very slowly through the riotous scene. When a few desperately broke individuals attempted to board the bus without paying, Rufus stood on the bottom step and crossed his arms. No one got on the bus. The frenzied crowd beat futilely on the corrugated sheet metal where the dog lay outstretched in mid-jump. The slow pace gave Bertie a chance to examine the controls in detail and to test a few hunches about levers and switches.

At last they passed through the outskirts of the city and into the desert. Bertie took his eyes away from the road to glance at his passenger. Rufus tried to look like a mean nigger, but by this time, Bertie had become something of a judge of character.

"What's up, Rufus?" Bertie asked.

"What you mean?"

"What do you think is happening? Has the whole world gone crazy?"

"Tell the truf, I don' know. I'd as soon not go back dere, dough."

"Good. Great. You can come with me!" Bertie cried.

"Where you goin'?"

"New York City, Rufus. The Big Apple."

"Dispatcher say St. Looie." Rufus glared at Bertie, but it was unconvincing after the excitement Bertie saw in the guard's eyes when he mentioned New York.

"Say, you ain't no damn bus driver, is you?"

"Nope," Bertie said with a smile, "I never said I was. He gave me the bus and I took it."

"You was wearin' de cap, dough."

"Somebody else gave that to me. I'm not saying I didn't fool them a little, but I've got to get to New York and I've got a valid ticket to San Francisco, so here I am. I've just been rerouted. And there you are. What now?"

"What you goin' New Yawk fo?"

"A good question, Rufus. If I told you, you probably wouldn't let me drive the bus."

"Try me," Rufus said, because he'd heard it in a movie once and it sounded like the right thing to say now.

"All right. There's a monkey there that wants to talk to me. Won't talk to anybody but me. I think it's from outer space or something, and it may know how to save the world."

"You and dis monkey gon' to save da worl'?"

"I didn't say that. I just have to talk to him."

"You know what I say? I say, anything is possible in dis crazy, fucked-up worl'. Lesgo to New Yawk City."

They were a little white Laurel and a big black Hardy. Bertie steered the impossibly large machine down the straight highway with a carefree ease. He hid his constant fear of crashing behind a manner that, for him, bordered on braggadocio. Once Rufus knew that Bertie wasn't a bus driver, his psychological hostility and childhood resentment passed, and Rufus saw the opportunity for friendship with the crazy white man.

"Know what my mother usen to say, Bertie?"

"What?"

"She said, 'We all los' souls. Dere is no balm in Gilead!' Know what dat mean?"

"I think so."

"Well, I wisht you'd tell me. I never could figure it out."

Thirty miles out of town they drove by an abandoned auto. After they passed it Bertie glanced into the rearview mirror on the passenger side of the bus and saw two forms huddled in the shadow of the car, hiding from the sun's heat. Bertie slowed the bus and carefully pulled it off the road.

"Rufus," he said, "I think those were kids."

"Dint' see no a-dults roun'."

"Let's go back and see." Bertie put on his padded hat to protect him from the sun, and because it was the only thing to identify him as a driver. There was a uniform jacket draped over the driver's seat, but it was seven sizes too large for Bertie. He and Rufus walked (Bertie would not risk backing the bus into a ditch) the hundred yards to the car. Two little black girls with identical pink dresses and shiny, blue plastic barrettes in their wavy, dark hair sat next to the car. Rufus, almost in tears, kneeled down in front of them.

"Whar's yo' daddy?"

They pointed out toward the desert, which stretched away into emptiness down a wide valley. No life was visible in the hazy distance.

"Why dint' you go with him?" Rufus asked.

"He didn't want us to," said the older girl.

"It was hot," said her sister, younger by a year or so. Then she added, "I'm so thirsty."

"Me too! I'm thirsty too." The older girl put her hand on Rufus's massive forearm. Rufus stood up, his face a vivid mixture of compassion for the girls and anger at their father. He took one by each hand and led them back to the bus. Bertie trailed behind, glancing occasionally out into the quiet vastness of the Nevada desert. By the time he climbed back into his seat behind the wheel, Rufus was already calling the girls by their names, Flora and Fawna. There was no water on the bus, but Rufus's lunch bag contained several carbonated colas, which the sisters happily drank.

The discovery of the two girls was the beginning of an impromptu rescue operation. As they drove through the next two hundred miles of arid wilderness, Bertie and Rufus picked up twenty-one more people. There was a steamfitter from Maryland, a tailor from Pittsburgh, a farm family from Missouri, and others, all with the same story: They'd lost everything in Vegas, they'd been harassed out of the city by police, they'd driven into the desert until they ran out of gas, and they had no idea what they were going to do next. These were not itinerants or criminals, but rather they were people like Bertie whose concern for the future had led them into rash acts.

Each new arrival carried onto the bus a few valued possessions. Bertie had learned by observation that when the bus was far from a terminal and needed fuel, it could be obtained through use of a plastic card kept in the visor clip in front of him. Toward the end of the day Rufus took up a collection and came up with nearly thirty-one dollars. He used this money to buy food: five pounds of hamburger, some pork links, buns, potato chips, and sodas. Just before dark, Bertie pulled the bus over in a Highway 40 rest area. The Sloats from Missouri had a barbecue set with them, someone else had a camp stove, and soon the happy smells of outdoor cooking rose around the picnic tables.

Everyone looked to Bertie for leadership. It was his bus, and he was the driver, and he had saved them all from perishing in the heat. That evening everyone got to know each other around a fire they built.

They scene had a quality reminiscent of dust bowl days. The sun set over the rest area in a blaze of orange and purple, made more radiant by radioactive fallout from recently resumed aboveground nuclear testing. There were no other travelers parked there. Trailer trucks, which normally would have crowded the lonely stopover, were moving only by day and in convoys with state police escorts, as a concession to mounting war hysteria.

"What we all need," someone said, "is a reason to go on."

"What's the point? It's all going to end soon, anyway."

"Not soon enough for us." The tailor spoke up.

"Yeah, it should have happened about three days ago when I dropped my last hundred at the blackjack table."

"No!" Bertie cried.

The group fell silent. Having lost everything material, they felt foolish and useless. Their will to live was no longer the strongest motivating factor in their existences.

"No! Listen to me." Bertie told them of his meeting with the ape at Big Boys Camp, his journey to New York, his unsuccessful search at the Bronx Zoo (he left out the part about Bellevue), and his recent phone conversation with Roscoe.

Some of his listeners were obviously skeptical. Others listened with rapt intent. After all, what else did they have? They had only Bertie and the bus. Bertie's tale, as improbable as it was, had the force of truth behind it, a strength that cannot be counterfeited.

The rest area was an oasis in the desert. Its tiny plot of grass was the only greenery, and its squat adobe rest rooms made the only shade and contained the only running water for fifty miles around. Later these forlorn outposts, like their historical counterparts in Arabia, would be fiercely contested prizes.

This night the Milky Way stretched like a white rainbow from horizon to horizon, a glowing belt that lit the moonless night with ancient power. When Bertie finished his recitation, there was a moment of silence.

"Who will join me?" Bertie asked.

"What can we do? You still haven't told us. . . ."

In truth Bertie had no idea how these people could help him, nor how he would feed them on their way across the country, nor did he have a clear notion of what he would do once he got to New York City. It was time for him to think on his feet.

"Well, uh, now you know I'm not a bus driver, yet here I've got all these passengers. I thought maybe you could pretend to be some group or other, and I could turn the sign to say 'Charter,' and, uh..." Bertie ran out of inspiration, but the people took up the idea with enthusiasm.

"Sure, great, who could we be?"

"How about... The Association of Las Vegas Losers, since that's what we are?"

"Naw, it's got to be realistic."

"Yeah, and sympathetic. Got to be something that everywhere we go, people will like us—"

"Maybe even feed us..." Bertie interjected.

"How about retirees? Everybody likes them."

"Depends on what they're retired from."

"Bakers!" somebody shouted.

"Doctors!" offered another, but this idea was hooted down by several people. Ministers, airline pilots, and some frivolous suggestions, such as parking-meter salesmen and barber-pole painters, were rejected before tiny Fawna came up with the winning entry.

"Santy Claus!" she cried.

So it was that Bertie set off the next morning with a hand-painted streamer taped over the dog on both sides of the bus: "Association of Retired Santa Clauses." Only nine of the twenty-one refugees from the previous day remained. Besides Rufus, Flora, and Fawna, there was the tailor, the five Ozark Sloats, a couple from California who were Bertie's most fervent supporters, and a young woman from Kansas. The others had disappeared. Some had hitched rides from the infrequent traffic. Others, Bertie feared, had been frightened

by his tale and had fled to the desert. There were unmistakable
signs that, for whatever reasons, despair had driven some to
fatal acts. By the edge of the oasis there were two pathetic
stacks of clothes and personal belongings, piled up the way
suicidal swimmers leave things at the water's edge. Bertie
gazed out into the desert for a long time before he was gently
persuaded by Rufus to come aboard the bus. The tailor was
already cutting down the previous driver's jacket; he needed
Bertie for a fitting.

11

Death of Tarzan

"It's hard to die when Mr. Tarzan is
around."

Liam O'Doul, in the 1939 film,
Tarzan's Secret Treasure.

Because Tarzan and Jane dwelt in a jungle paradise, an escarpment high above the African plain, and because they were at one with Nature like races of old, they lived to great age like Biblical characters. Boy went to live in civilization and came back a fatigued old man while his parents were still in their prime. They went through seven generations of Cheetahs. Over the last twenty or thirty years they had become slightly less active, and as many old people do, they took up farming with a bit of acreage near the tree house. Tarzan didn't swing on vines and creepers anymore. He strolled through the jungle with a slight limp from his last encounter with mad bull elephants, or perhaps it was crocodiles, he couldn't quite remember which.

One morning Tarzan found Jane sprawled under a baobab

tree, her primitive rake still in her hand. She had fallen asleep
and died. Tarzan took her body and buried it next to Boy's,
who had died some years previous. He made a cross for her
grave. He knew she would want it, although he didn't understand why, and later on he held his own ritual procession,
calling the animals of the jungle one by one to pay homage
to her spirit. The dark forest mourned.

After this sorrow Tarzan could stay alone no longer. He
sought out the company of men—he, who had been a recluse.
He wanted to speak to someone before he left the world. He
dressed in an old English tweed suit that Jane had bought for
him many years ago and set out for the City of Men.

The city he knew seventy years ago no longer existed. It
had been an African gold-rush city, and it had faded rapidly
into jungle. Ten miles up the coast, however, there was Suntown, a European resort community. It lay at the far reaches
of a shallow bay ringed by a stretch of glittering white sand.
Sixty years had passed since Tarzan had seen the ocean. Its
immensity did not overwhelm him; the African veldt was as
vast as in his imagination. Its colors fascinated him: azure
blue and agate green, shifting and changing on wind and tide
and sun and clouds.

The figure that strode into Suntown soon became a spectacle, an object of awe, derision, and much speculation. Tarzan's white beard and swept-back mane made some people
think of Noah, or even God. Children followed him down
the streets. They poked and pulled at the latest Cheetah until
she was compelled to jump up on Tarzan's shoulder.

Suntown was one huge red-light district. The sidewalks
were lined with beautiful black women in outrageous cos-
tumes and makeup. Pornographic movie houses and live sex
theaters were the predominant attractions for the thrill-starved
soldiers and government workers who made up the majority
of the vacationers. As in Las Vegas, recent world events had
intensified the atmosphere of desiccation and debauchery.

Two frightened soldiers confronted him. Tarzan took their rifles and smashed them against a nearby tree, as he used to do in the old days, and he shook the men and made them run away. Then he continued his walk. After a little while the pavement grew too hot for his bare feet, so he outran the children and curious followers and made his way to the beach.

"Ocean good, men bad," Tarzan muttered to himself. His voice cracked from disuse, and he realized that he no longer wanted any discourse with men. He had seen what they had come to. It was not far from what he expected, he thought, remembering his earlier contact with them.

He threw off his shirt and tweed jacket and pants and lay naked on the sand; his ancient body would have been the envy of many a middle-aged man. Cheetah played with sticks and beach glass. She never strayed more than a few yards from her master.

Just as Tarzan fell asleep, a commotion awoke him. A jeep shooting rooster tails of sand behind it hurtled toward him. Ten armed men clung to the vehicle's seats and perched on fenders.

Tarzan disdained to look at them. In the old times odds of ten or twenty to one would not have discouraged him. He did not anguish over the many reasons for living, as modern man would; instead, he made his choice like an animal. He could stand and fight, killing before he was killed in battle, or he could go off and die alone. He thought briefly of the abandoned tree house and the two graves, and he measured his strength. The armed group left their jeep and approached with stealthy, timid steps. Tarzan cleared his throat and let loose a final call of the jungle. The trumpeting yell stopped traffic a mile away in Suntown. Flocks of birds rose from the forest, screeching and swooping. He took up Cheetah and held her before him. "Tarzan go, Cheetah stay." The chimp made noises of complaint, but no animal could refuse a command from the Lord of the Jungle. They hugged and caressed each other's heads, then Cheetah ran off to a tree at the edge of the sand. Tarzan turned toward the water and ran, diving forward when he was waist-deep. He moved with strong, smooth strokes. There was something deep inside him, a strange predilection for swimming.

The men by the jeep jumped up and rushed at Tarzan, but they were too late. Their bullets splatted harmlessly around him, and soon they stopped firing. They watched, pointing and gesticulating, as he disappeared from view, swimming directly away from shore. The soldiers seemed to understand that they had been witness to an extraordinary event. They stood silent for a few minutes, then they climbed into the car and drove away. Cheetah scampered down to the water's edge. With her superior animal eyesight she could still make out the trail of white foam from Tarzan's powerful leg kicks, but she made no effort to follow him. At sunset she left the beach.

Cheetah was not a wild animal. As successive generations of chimpanzees adapted to life with Tarzan and Jane, each became less feral. The current Cheetah was a highly intelligent specimen. Although Tarzan frowned upon it, Jane had worked with the chimps until they could talk. In fact, some of them had more extensive vocabularies and a better command of the rules of grammar than Tarzan, who, of course, had been raised by apes and had therefore learned English as a second language after he was an adult. It was the chimps' secret with Jane, and they never used their talents around Tarzan lest they cause a domestic disturbance. Now that her masters were gone, Cheetah was in the midst of an identity crisis. She knew that she belonged with her kind, yet another part of her craved the tea and small talk she had shared with Jane.

Her first attempts at social interaction with the humans of Suntown were miserable failures. She approached an old black native who was boiling water over a small brazier outside her miserable shanty at the edge of Suntown.

"Makin' a spot o' tea, dearie?" Cheetah asked, in the queer Cockney that Jane had taught her. The woman shrieked and tottered away. After a few such efforts Cheetah was about to give up when she met a friend, one who talked just like herself. He was a former British Navy man, now a Merchant Marine. He had owned a few parrots in his time, but until Cheetah hailed him, he had never heard a monkey talk.

"Spare a bite o' yer crumpet, mate?" she croaked from the bushes where she was hiding. The sailor looked around but saw no one. He scratched his head and walked on. Cheetah called to him again.

"Caw! 'Ow 'bout it, laddie? A crust for an ol' girl?"

Jane had taught the earlier Cheetahs correct English (albeit with an American accent). Later she had wanted variety, so she'd made them talk as if they were fishmongers and sailors.

The sailor located Cheetah the second time he heard her. With a little bit of coaxing he was able to draw her out of her hiding place. Soon they were getting along famously, drinking gin in the sailor's hotel room.

When Cheetah found herself in a cell the next morning, she knew what had happened. The sailor had gotten her drunk and sold her to a man who bought animals for carnivals. This man thought he had himself a real find, a talking chimp. He was sure he'd been sober the night before when the inebriated animal sang and slurred an astounding litany of antiquated Cockney slang.

When Cheetah refused to repeat her performance of the previous night, the animal dealer figured he'd been tricked, and he sold Cheetah to a zoo instead of a carnival. Cheetah had learned her lesson. She kept her mouth shut, and if she hadn't met Vith Pankas, she might never have spoken again.

12

Voice and Articulation

Vith Pankas could have destroyed the world anytime he wanted. Three million years ago scientists on his planet had invented molecular spectrolizers, nefarious weapons that instantly reduced matter to its organic components. If you shot a human being with one, you'd get a puddle of mineral-rich salt water.

Vith was teaching an unauthorized night class at the Bronx Zoo. Though its title was "Voice and Articulation," the class often resembled civics or social studies. Vith was a one-man prisoner-support group. He zipped around the world during the day, and in the evening he brought his pupils their favorite treats and read them the newspaper. News of the world was avidly discussed by his students. Reports of the buffalos' demonstration, for example, caused a sensation, and many of his eager students made extracurricular reports.

Vith was a medium in the true sense of the word. Through him or, more accurately, through what he called his communion field, the animals were able to converse with him and with each other even if they were a mile apart. In fact, Vith's communion field could stretch across the cosmos.

One night, as Vith set up his communion field for class, he was surprised to find that one of the creatures did some rudimentary thinking in strange, broken English. At first he thought that a human being had somehow wandered into the field, then he realized that it was a chimpanzee in the ape house. Locked doors were no barrier to one who circumnavigated the globe daily. Vith entered the row of cages and found Cheetah huddled in one corner of the cage's squalor. She was panic-stricken and depressed.

"Greetings, chimp. How do you come by your English?"

"Me master waz Tarzan, the Ape Man, yer honor."

"Tarzan was a character in a book. He was not real."

"True enough, yer honor. But they waz many a gentleman as fancied the jungle life, and ladies too. Oi heard of as many as twenty sech Tarzans, an' near as many Janes. Oi loved 'em both, y'know."

Vith scanned the chimp's elementary memory banks and quickly learned her story. That morning Cheetah had been transferred to the Bronx Zoo from another zoo where she'd created a sensation by weaving small baskets and working at the other crafts Jane had taught her, trying to make her cage more homelike.

Vith performed some simple psychic surgery to correct Cheetah's unfortunate lower-class dialect. In keeping with the cyclical nature of things, he gave her the accent and vocabulary of a lady of the manor.

"Yes, much better." Cheetah recognized the change and its source at once. She nodded graciously to Vith and thanked her benefactor. "You've a modest talent for transubstantiation, young man." Vith bowed in return. "It appears you were about to conduct some sort of class. Please, don't let me interrupt." Cheetah seated herself on a concrete block, legs crossed at her ankles, hands folded in her lap.

"This is a wire service filler story that will interest everyone," Vith announced to his class. "Listen. 'Nairobi, Kenya.

Professor Orville McMaster of Kenya's Wildlife Preservation
Group stated today that species continue to become extinct
at an alarming rate, which has increased from two species a
day to ten species a day in just five years. Although there
remain some five hundred thousand species, the trend is toward general extinction. Professor McMaster is working on
the theory that in some cases the animals seem to be actively
eradicating themselves, pointing to the recent epidemic of
whale beachings as an example. He adds that in many cases
it is as if species are choosing extinction rather than waiting
to suffer their fate at the hands of humans."

"Oh, Whales, ancient Brothers, that is not the way!" the
elephants trumpeted, for the animals often spoke in their own
languages during class. Lately the zoo had been raucous in
the evening from the calls, cries, and yowls of the animals.
It upset the zookeepers and the neighborhood.

"Anything to shake the humans out of their lethargy," Vith
said. "We all agree that suicide is not the way, but what
valiance!"

"We want to fight," the lions roared, and on Bronx Park
East, families cringed in their living rooms and checked the
triple dead-bolt locks on their doors. "Why don't you let us
out, Vith Pankas?"

"Let us out! We're coming out!" the menagerie sent up a
cacophony of protest.

Vith quieted them. "Where would you go? Captivity has
made you weak. You have a greater contribution to make
here."

"I know a teasing brat or two I could make a meal of," a
panther snarled. There was a round of growled assent.

"Remember your lessons, Savage Ones. 'The meek shall
inherit the earth.' You must learn to curb your violent natures.
Truly you are not much better than these humans. Look to
your gentle brothers, the vegetarians: the buffalo, rhinoceros,
hippopotamus, deer, and ox."

"Ox," the musk ox sniffed. "I hope you mean us and not those dirty beasts of burden. To serve man, pooh, what a humiliation."

As there were no oxen to present their case, Vith replied, "Who has put you all here?"

There was no need for an answer.

"Let us out, Vith Pankas!" The lament rose again. Vith was firm.

"There is no place I can take you where you would be safe. But you can do this one thing. With my help you can demonstrate conclusively to them that Nature is aware. Nature knows. We'll show them that."

"Excuse me, Vith."

"Yes, Miss Cheetah."

"How do you plan to show those dreadful humans?"

"Well, Miss Cheetah, I'm a prankster, you know, and I'm setting up a little consciousness-raising exhibition on Zoo Day, next Saturday. You could be my star actress!" Vith brightened as the thought came to him. His clothes and skin turned from deep brown to tan, then faded and darkened until he resumed his original one-color self. "Yes! I can see it now. Will you help us, Miss Cheetah?"

"I am in your debt, sir." The chimp stood and did a precious imitation of an elderly dame's curtsy. "What is the play and what is my role?"

Vith described his idea. He had chosen a perfect day for the demonstration, Zoo Day, a week away. The mayor would be there. All the TV stations would be covering it as a human-interest piece. It would be a perfect opportunity for a splashy act of media theater. Zoo security people were preoccupied with precautions for the mayor's visit. They were unprepared for the rally Vith organized.

Preparations continued all week, both inside and outside the cages of the Bronx Zoo. Park workers built a grandstand in the central plaza. Others cleaned cages and whitewashed the graffiti-scarred walls. (Recently the fad for spray-painting slogans in impossible places had reached new levels of boldness. Ten-year-olds, pressurized cans in hand, were found scaling skyscrapers on Wall Street. At the zoo the cages of the big cats were coveted trophies. There had been casualties on both sides.) The animals practiced nightly for Vith's production. He rewrote the script to include Miss Cheetah, who handled her duties like a veteran.

At last the day arrived. A throng gathered outside the gates of the zoo early in the morning. New Yorkers had not permitted themselves the extremes of abandonment seen in Las Vegas, but every theater, movie house, sports team, racetrack, and whorehouse was doing record business. Events like Zoo Day or Chinese New Year became mob scenes.

When the zoo opened at ten that morning, the animals stomped and shivered nervously. In streamed a crowd at least five times as large as the previous record attendance. Soon every cage had a crowd seven and eight deep surrounding it. From a hidden place near the grandstand Vith sang to the frightened creatures in calm and assuring tones inaudible to human ears. Loudspeakers were strung through the park. Over them came waves of poorly played and imperfectly recorded calliope music, drenching the air with steamy wheezing. The effect was maddening, especially to the sensitive ears of many animals. They cowered in the center of their cages, away from hundreds of outstretched, intruding arms. Eventually the festivities started; the crowd left the beleaguered, paranoid beasts and gathered in front of the central stage. Vith was able to comfort the animals.

"Now, then, my friends, easy, easy. The worst part is over. When we finish, they'll clear out, believe me. Rest easy now. Your part comes later."

The ceremony consisted of boring speeches given by people completely unconnected to the zoo. Yet the crowd listened with interest and applauded the crass political pitches made in the name of the zoo. They longed for a sense of continuity that was increasingly hard to affirm, as a feeling of crisis clouded the horizon of the future. Parades, meaningless sporting events, and ceremonies like today's were symbols of faith.

At one end of the planned speeches Vith led Miss Cheetah up the steps of the stage and to the podium, just as the mayor was thanking everyone for coming. Vith whispered a few words to the mayor, who laughed and turned back to the microphone.

"It seems that the animal world is represented today by this chimpanzee, who has a few words to say. After all, it is their day." With that, he stepped back from the microphone, confidently expecting to witness a clever bit of ventriloquism by the chimp's trainer in the oddly drab outfit. This episode had taken the mayor by surprise, but he assumed it was planned by the zoo staff and his aides, who never consulted him, anyway. He thought the publicity would be cute and happily stood aside for Miss Cheetah. She adroitly adjusted the gooseneck microphone to her level. The crowd quieted, unsure of what to expect.

"Good afternoon." Miss Cheetah's aristocratic accent drew some laughter, but the crowd watched intently. Vith kept his mouth tightly shut.

"I come to you today with a plea from all of us here. We are your prisoners, it is true. Yet in a greater sense you are your own prisoners."

Bertie would have recognized the strange scene: Once again a lower primate lectured to its higher, more evolved form.

"Are you happy today?" Miss Cheetah continued, "or do you feel that something is terribly wrong? This is a festival day. Why is there no joy, only fear? You know the answer. War approaches. If there is anyone in this crowd who has the power to stop it, please do so at once. You could all stop it, each and every one of you, if only your hearts were right.

Oh, but I am afraid for you. All of use, those you kill and maim, those whose homes you have bulldozed, flooded, burned, and otherwise destroyed to make way for yourselves, whose air and water you have poisoned, we are all afraid for you. Why is this? Because you are one of us. Too long you have denied this. It is time to show you. First, however, a personal message." Miss Cheetah dropped her voice to low, confidential tones.

"Vith has asked me to say that if any of you see dear Bertie Rupp, please tell him that Vith would like to see him at the zoo. He was out of the galaxy when Bertie called, or he certainly would have greeted him, and he apologizes for the inconvenience.

"Now," she continued, resuming her oratorical air, "*hear our plea!*"

With that cry she leapt on Vith's shoulders, and with a conductor's flourish she raised her elongated chimpanzee arms and gave the signal for the start. From the cages, pens, pools, and yards of the animals came an assortment of bellows, screeches, hoots, and cackles. At first it sounded like mere noise, but as Vith turned up the resonating communion field, people in the stunned audience heard the chanted song: "We shall overcome."

The choice of words was another example of Vithian humor. He felt that it was poignant and appropriate. The chant grew louder: "We shall overcome someday."

The crowd panicked and ran for the exits, as Vith had predicted. Miss Cheetah was grabbed by alert authorities, but Vith, of course, got away, and he saw to it that the chimp would not be harmed. The police were unable to suppress all of the videotape taken by newsmen, but a curious thing happened when station technicians reran the footage: the sounds of the chant tape were indecipherable as anything except what they were, noises of highly agitated beasts. The speech apparently given by the female chimpanzee was still under-standable.

Local and federal agencies fought for the chance to handle the investigation, and the Federal Bureau of Investigation won. No one from the FBI believed the chimp's story. Miss Cheetah had been quite talkative since her capture. Seventeen agents of various levels of importance insisted upon inter-rogating her. She told the exact truth: that she had been Tarzan's, that Tarzan was dead and now she was Vith's, the man from outer space who had organized the spectacle at Zoo Day.

No one believed her story. Naturally the government peo-ple were convinced she was an instrument of the enemy. Miss Cheetah held firm. She told the truth at all times, which baffled and confounded her interrogators. The authorities de-cided to put out the word that the whole thing had been a hoax, that the chimp couldn't talk at all.

That night, in her isolated quarters in an experimental lab near the zoo, Cheetah could hear via the communion field the satisfied grunts of the animals as Vith read them news-paper accounts of the day's excitement.

13

Emily

When the six-o'clock bell rang, Emily had to stop praying. No matter how close she was to God, not even if she felt His hand brush across her face, could she miss six-fifteen vespers. She was second soprano in a choir that was modestly famous for their renditions of medieval chants and hymns. One never knew when Father Scotius might have important guests, potential benefactors, to be charmed by the music. And, of course, the choir served God. It was her duty to sing in the service.

Not that she had frequent visits from God. In fact, He was elusive, mysterious, distant. She tried to get to know Him. She labored to get close to His son, Jesus. Opening her heart to Him, she revealed her innermost secrets, those intimacies of the soul that a woman rarely tells her mother and almost never confides to her husband. But there were problems. She could never see how Jesus could do for her what she felt each person must do for himself—that is, forgive sins and save the world.

She didn't know how to be a supplicant, as the severe elder sisters often reminded her. She lacked humility, they said, but that wasn't right, because she had learned the spirit of submission on the long road that had brought her to this California farm.

Emily straightened her hair: at least she had learned to do this without a mirror. If only she could remove the barrier that kept her from God so easily. Every waking moment she considered how to get nearer to Him. It was this kind of intense devotion that kept her from a normal life in the outside world, where it was impossible to concentrate. Sometimes, though, Emily wondered if there weren't more distractions here at the commune.

There was chapel seven times a day, choir practices, required attendance at all meals, and seemingly endless meetings for projects the group promoted. Father Scotius was an activist. The commune mirrored the personality of its founder. Sometimes Emily felt that the only times she really had to herself were the moments she spent with the horse. She would start a good grooming and allow herself to fall into the rhythm of the exercise, a hundred patient strokes of the mane or tail, and it would seem to her that she could learn something from the calm, accepting demeanor of the animal. The earthy smell of the stable and the powerful sensuality of the mare's chest and flanks kept her from slipping out of touch entirely with the real things of the world.

Father Scotius had created a monastery, and the atmosphere was oppressive. When Emily watched the mare's stud nuzzle her and then mount her with eyes as wild as only a horse's can be, she felt nothing, and it troubled her. The huggy-feely Californians in the group gave off a wooden, neutral, asexual feeling when they touched her. She hated it.

Why did she stay, then? Partly to be sheltered from the insanities and depravities of the world at the end of the road where the sign read, HEAVEN'S GATE ¼ MI. Then again, it was also the father who kept her here, by the force of his will. Until she understood what it was about Father Scotius that fascinated her, she couldn't leave. She thought he must be either a saint or a devil to have so many people on this earth abiding by his will, living under his sway.

Emily first met the father when he gave a talk at her Newman Club in college. She was impressed with the vitality of his program, its combination of social action and spiritual renewal. Over her college career she spent much time at the monastery, and when she graduated, she took a job in a small town nearby so that she could continue to attend the weekend retreats.

One weekend she accompanied some of the sisters when they visited a migrant workers' shantytown in the San Joaquin Valley, just an hour drive from the commune in the foothills of the Sierras. They were on one of their missions of mercy, bringing food and spiritual succor to the indigent farm workers. The devout Mexican Catholics were an easy audience for the nuns. They ate the home-baked pies and cakes with delight, and most listened obediently to the sisters' homilies.

The cluster of corrugated tin and tar-paper shacks where the itinerants lived was right in the middle of the fields, down a dirt road on private land, well away from the prying eyes of government inspectors or nosy passersby. There was no electricity, no flush toilets, and no piped gas, only kerosene or butane tanks. The flimsy homes broiled in the daytime and were chilly on cold nights.

To one side was a mound of refuse that was torched from time to time, giving off that pungent smell of burning trash. The younger men were gathered there, drinking beers, not taking part. Because Emily was younger than the sisters, she decided to reach out to the youths in a ministry. Unlike the others, she did not wear the full-length habit of the order. She still dressed as a demure college student from Kansas. Her embroidered peasant blouse and blue jeans showed off her trim figure. The top was like something a Sonoran girl might wear, except it cost thirty dollars and was of fine cotton instead of rough weave. Since she was not dressed as a nun, the Mexican men saw no reason to treat her with respect.

"Aiyee! What finery!"

"Olà! Señorita! Welcome to our beautiful homes."

"You have come to see how the poor people live, no?"

Someone said something in Spanish about her breasts, and the men laughed at her. Emily blushed even though she didn't understand the remark.

"Hey! Get Jesus out here! He should see this." Others took up the cry.

"Jesus! Come out! There is a sister here to see you."

From inside the shack nearest the trash heap came a fiery outburst of profane Spanish. Emily blushed again. She was glad the nuns were far enough away to have missed the obscenities, several of which clearly referred to the Catholic Church. Now she was angry. She stamped her foot.

"That's no way to talk. You ought to be ashamed of yourselves, hiding behind closed doors. You wouldn't talk that way to my face."

"You want to bet?" somebody spoke from the vague shadows of the smoky fire.

"He is not like his namesake, this Jesus! Oh, no!" another told her with melodic sarcasm.

"Hey, Jesus! Come out! This sister wants to save your bastard soul!"

The men around the fire were enjoying Emily's awkwardness and embarrassed uncertainty, but there was nothing malicious in their actions. When Jesus opened the door, they stepped back. Apparently they had not expected him to appear. He was a beautiful man, Emily observed, handsome in the Latin way. He had a bottle of tequila in one hand and a half-sucked lemon in the other, and his first words to Emily were more vile than his previous curses. Emily was beyond blushing. She lost her composure before his dark stare and had turned to leave when he called her back.

"Don't walk away when I'm talking to you, bitch. It's impolite."

She came back. "You're right," she said. "I'm sorry." She waited for him to continue, but he let her stand there, not leaving and not really staying.

"Do you really think you could save the soul of one so lost as me?" Jesus finally asked.

"If you would show your true self to me, instead of acting so mean—" Emily began, but Jesus threw the lemon at her and cocked the quart of tequila as if it were going to follow. Emily shrieked and ducked, but Jesus only laughed and took a drink from the upraised bottle.

"I'll show you. Just come inside my home here and I'll show you everything. I'll show you Paradise, eh, *hombres*?" Emily ran away crying.

Two days later she was walking to her job in town when she saw Jesus waiting for her by his car, an ugly old Chevy Biscayne with too much chrome in the wrong places and a layer of farm dust so thick, it looked like a coat of paint. He was all smiles and apologies, claiming drunkenness, which was certainly true, and offered to make it up to her by buying her dinner. She accepted.

He took her to a small place in the poor Mexican district of the college town. She noticed that he had made a definite effort to dress up for the occasion. His black hair was slicked back, his jeans were ironed, and he wore a fancy Western shirt with sequins, embroidery, and pearl buttons. She was pleased that he treated her as his date, opening the car door and restaurant door for her, ordering her drinks and dinner, and attempting to charm her in every way.

For her part, Emily still wanted to work on Jesus' soul, but she was feeling the attractions of the handsome Mexican and the excitement of her introduction to his culture. She drank her first margaritas and ate her first real Mexican meal.

When he had thoroughly seduced her heart, Jesus took her to a motel and overwhelmed her with powerful lovemaking.

A week later Emily had quit her job, left her volunteer work with the nuns, and gone off with Jesus, following the harvests, living in shantytowns. Two months later the beatings began. At first Emily thought it was just because Jesus drank. Then she began to doubt herself. Had she displeased him so that he had to hit her?

They were thrown off several farms when Emily couldn't hide a black eye or a swollen cheekbone. Several kindly farmers and their wives took Emily aside and tried to dissuade her from following him, but she was blind with love. Nightly she prayed aloud for his soul. This enraged him and brought on further beatings.

One night Jesus was killed in a bar fight, and Emily's ordeal was over. Yet because she had not done anything to free herself, she was not really free. They were in Texas working on the cotton crop when he didn't come back one night from a drinking spree in the cantinas. The sheriff who picked her up to identify the body took pity on her and offered her a bus ticket to anywhere. She fled to the monastery.

That was two years ago. Emily still didn't go with the others on their evangelistic forays. Instead, she did the more unpleasant chores, cleaning the bathrooms and sweeping.

Gradually her time with Jesus had become like a forgotten existence, like a dream, like another lifetime or a story she had heard. Always she tried to keep the true Jesus separate from his evil namesake, but it was hard and sometimes she got confused.

Father Scotius didn't make things any easier. Not that the father had ever been lewd or suggestive to her. On the contrary, he was always the soul of kindness, keeping the story of her past a secret.

Why was she here? Why did she stay? These questions intruded on her meditations. As time went by and they remained unanswered, the daily rituals that used to be distractions became comfortable, even necessary parts of her day. She loved to sing, which was fortunate since she got the opportunity seven times a day. Singing and brushing the horses: These were her two meditations. The endless repetitions of Latin prayers did nothing for her.

Once again it was time for vespers. Emily straightened her habit and adjusted the coif and veil over her short-cropped hair. Once, she remembered, she'd had a long mane like the horse's to comb out nightly. Even with her cropped hair she was a Midwestern beauty, her pink skin glowing, her eyes soft and full of spirituality. Jesus, she thought, where are you? Her life suddenly seemed purposeless and unfulfilled. How could she ask Jesus to help when she couldn't help herself?

She knew what Father Scotius would say. "You must let him do it for you. It's so easy! He will take your troubles on Himself. He will absolve your sins. He will cleanse your soul."

But how? thought Emily. *How? How can that be? How can anyone do for me what I have to do on my own?* This was the root question of her existence, she decided. She would go to Father Scotius's rectory that night and ask him for guidance. He would be too busy with the guests after services.

Sneaking around after lights-out in the monastery was a silly thing to do, but Emily was determined to get the answer to the burning question of her glowing heart. The rectory was set apart from the farmhouses and converted barns that comprised the main area of the monastery. It sat on a hill above the other buildings, farther from the main road. There was a dirt road leading up to the front door and looping to make a carriage turnaround, and there was a path that led along the side of the hill to the back door.

Emily walked along the path, hoping to avoid being seen,

but as she climbed toward the father's house she saw to her horror that someone was descending the same way. Feeling foolish and childish, she scurried behind some bushes.

Sister B came down the path past her, dressed in her nightclothes. The odor of alcohol and the strong smell of recent sex emanated so pungently from Sister B that Emily had to suppress a bawdy laugh.

It seemed absurd now to continue on. What had happened was so transparent; yet Emily went on, even abandoning the circuitous path when she saw a light on in the front room. She marched up to the door and rang the bell. Father Scotius opened it. He was dressed in a bathrobe, and his face was flushed.

"Sister E! What a surprise. Come in."

"You said we could visit you whenever we had a spiritual problem. . . ."

"Of course, of course, come in." Father Scotius discreetly closed the door to his living quarters and shepherded Emily to the parlor where he held weekly teas with select members of the nunnery. Perhaps it was at one of these sessions that Sister B had arranged her liaison, Emily thought.

"I often find myself thinking about your teachings," Emily began.

"Excellent, excellent, I want to be provocative," Father Scotius replied.

"Yes, but there's one thing I don't understand."

"What's that?"

"It's been a problem all along for me. I can accept so much of what you say, what the Bible says. like when Jesus says 'The kingdom of Heaven is within you—'"

"Yes, Sister, yes—"

"But I don't see how he can take my sins from me."

"Have you come to him in earnest, with head bowed, saying 'Jesus, take me'?"

"Yes, Father, I have."

"You must try harder."

But it seems to me that I have to change, not Jesus change me."

"Sister E . . ."

"Yes?"

"Come over here." Father Scotius gestured for her to join him on the couch where he lay with the casual unselfconsciousness of a drunk.

"Sit down, my dear." She sat at his feet at the far end of the couch. He leered at her. "What do you think is the meaning of the life and death of Jesus?"

"I don't know. I suppose that's my question."

"Sister E, many people misunderstand one of the main elements in the life story of Jesus: his conception. Why did God have sex with a woman? Why didn't he just send Jesus? Why have him born of woman?"

"I don't know."

"The fact that Jesus was celibate, that his life was a demonstration of purity, reverence, and kindness: That's what you cling to, isn't it?"

"Yes," Emily answered. Her voice was flat and dull. This wasn't the answer she wanted. Father Scotius struggled to sit up, his loose robe falling open. He took her hands as if to comfort her, and he put his puffy face close to hers. His degradation was complete now in her eyes.

"Yes, well, concentrate on the other part. His conception shows us that God is a living, active principle. He is dynamic. That's the way to paradise. I'll show you . . ."

The father was stroking her hand with his, but he had chosen the wrong words. They echoed those the other Jesus had used to insult her when they first met. Now, two years after his death, Emily chose to free herself.

"Let go of me." Emily stood up. "I'll be leaving now."

"Isn't that what you came for?" the father asked her cruelly.

"Go to hell!" Emily shouted. She ran out of the house and

down the hill, not caring if she made noise or who saw her. When she got to her dormitory, she packed, leaving behind the habit, taking only her underwear and wearing the clothes she had arrived in.

14

Sex Life of the Adult Rupp

Bertie and his gang of twelve were in Coldwater, Kansas, when he found a week-old copy of *The New York Times* with a story about Zoo Day. They had come here to Coldwater because the woman from Kansas, Emily Butterworth, thought she could hide the group for a little while on her parents' farm. They had been five days on the road. Everybody was frazzled, especially Bertie, who had done all the driving. Rufus had become the most popular Santa Claus, but he smelled too bad to be effective at the moment.

Bertie was the least popular Santa. He was too scrawny, and besides, he just didn't have the ho-ho-ho for the job. Rufus, however, was resplendent in a white cotton beard and a red-and-black outfit the tailor assembled. Flora and Fawna were conscripted as elves, and they played their parts with sparkle and flair. In several towns church groups or civic organizations arranged meals for the troupe, or sympathetic diners picked up their tab. Retired Santa Clauses gave people the same kind of reassurance as baseball playoffs or Zoo Days.

The Butterworth farm was outside of Coldwater, just sixty

miles down the road from Plains. If Bertie had only known how close he was to the trigger point of all his fears, he would have repeated the heroic effort of the buffalo, but his memories of those days in Bellevue were vague and imprecise. He was sure of what he had seen, but never could have found the place.

The Butterworths owned a wheat farm. The Rupp place had been a corn farm, but the elements were the same. Emily's parents were walking, talking American characters. Mrs. Butterworth was just like Dorothy's Auntie Em in *The Wizard of Oz*. She baked buttermilk biscuits the morning they arrived, and she acted like Emily always brought a dozen ragged strangers home for breakfast.

"How have you been, dear?" she asked Emily, wiping her hands on her checkered apron. "We haven't heard from you. Are you still with that church group?"

Emily gave her mother a tense smile.

"No, Mother, I'm on my own now. I've been living in California for a while . . . oh, but you don't want to hear this!" She cut herself off abruptly.

Bertie changed the subject by reading the article about Zoo Day, but his interest in the quiet woman was heightened. He realized that he knew very little about her. While the other members of the group had quickly become friends, she had remained distant.

Ozark and Rimaldi Sloat were pleasant, gregarious people who belied the image of those mountain people as strange and dangerous. They hit it off immediately with the Butterworths. Ozark had an opinion about everything, from the best shape for an ax handle to why the great globe is round. Emily's father held equally firm convictions, and the two men had a wonderful conversation, neither listening to the other, and each convinced that the other agreed with him.

Ruben, Spence, and Ozark, Jr., were well-mannered, curious boys. They didn't play much with Flora and Fawna,

who rarely left Rufus's side, but they didn't tease them, and
Junior whittled them some dolls from clothespins with his
buck knife.

The tailor introduced himself as Ben Braun. He wore a
belt. Unlike the belt in the fairy tale, this one didn't boast
"Seven with One Blow," but it did have a slogan. Embroidered in gold thread on a broad velvet band were the words:
"A Stitch in Time Saved Nine." At the breakfast table the
tailor leaned back to pat his extensive belly, exposing the belt
in its shining splendor.

" 'A Stitch in Time Saved Nine.' What does that mean?"
Bertie asked.

"I was hoping you'd ask. In my spare time I'm a parachute
mender."

"Do you jump, yourself?" Bertie wondered.

"Never!" said Ben with a note of unmistakable finality.

Emily laughed. Her mother noticed this and blushed. Bertie beamed.

The California couple chimed in with laughter like a pair
of matched bells. Del and Bryce were chutists.They were
married on a jump and plummeted to a reception at the drop
site. They were also enthusiastic hang-glider pilots. When
they weren't surfing in New Zealand or Hawaii, they lived
on their houseboat in the Sausalito harbor. Two weeks ago
Del bet an ace-high nothing hand in Las Vegas and lost the
boat to a pair of deuces. California-style born-again Christians, Del and Bryce had been preparing for The End for a
long time. As Del put it, they wanted to be "where the action
is." Bertie's fantastic story seized their imagination, and they
followed him. Three years ago they had spent two months
and several thousand dollars following a confidence man who
claimed to be from outer space, recruiting people (and col-
lecting their money) for a new colony on Cygnus 7.

Plates of eggs and biscuits, jugs of gravy, and bottles of
milk crowded the tabletop. As dishes were emptied, they

were swept off by Mrs. Butterworth and others brought on. When breakfast was over, most of the people went out to the barn to sleep on the warm, aromatic hay. Bertie asked Emily if she would show him the farm.

Bertie was like the earth, solid and impassive on the surface; bubbling, molten, pressurized energy at the core. He was the classic absentminded professor. In the old days he could start thinking about a problem one afternoon in the lab and wake up weeks or months later with the answer.

The single-pointedness of mind attained by scientists and monks is not within the realm of experience of most humans; it is an extreme. For ordinary people who think about sex all the time it is hard to conceive a state of mind where the libido is not the central drive of life. For Bertie, who had been both a scientist and a monk of sorts, sex had not been the dominant motivator.

Perhaps it was the feel of dirt beneath his feet, or the fragrance of the wheat undulating in all directions to the horizon, but he remembered first seeing Emily standing, with the expression of a jilted Madonna, next to her broken-down automobile in the desert.

She and Bertie were kindred spirits. They walked the fields together.

"The world is so horrible, Bertie. I joined a group to get away, and it worked. But one day I was in the chapel at the retreat and I thought to myself, this isn't real. I'm not even living. Everybody has forgotten about me. So I left. I went to live by the ocean, then a few weeks ago I felt like I had to see my parents again, but my car broke down before I got there, and that's when you showed up. . . ."

"Emily, if you're looking for reality, it's bad luck for you to meet me. . . ."

"What do you mean, Bertie?"

"Well, you must've thought that story I told was pretty crazy. . . ."

"Funny thing is, Bertie, I believed you. Shouldn't I?"

"Oh, yes, everything I said is true. It's just not very real. I believe it myself, but remember, I lived at Bellevue."

They looked at each other through understanding eyes.

"So what's next?" Emily asked.

"I don't think there's much next left, for most people," Bertie replied.

They talked about their lives, their separate searches for religious truth, Emily's time at the retreat, Bertie's long odyssey in pursuit of himself. They held hands tentatively, almost unconsciously.

"We prayed seven times a day in that place, Bertie. We dressed up in nun's habits even though we weren't nuns, and there was nobody around to see us, anyway. We had our own rooms, like cells, with a bare mattress on the floor and an old blanket for bedding. And . . . oh, Bertie if I tell you all this, you won't like me anymore. . . ."

"I'll like you, I'll like you!"

"Remember a little while ago when I told you how I realized I was wasting my life there, so I left?"

"Yes?"

"That's not the way it happened. I wanted to stay but I couldn't."

"What do you mean? Did they kick you out or something?"

"Oh, no. Everybody's always so supportive, it gets sickening. I mean, everybody hugs everybody all the time. It gets so it doesn't mean anything."

"Is that why you left?" Bertie asked.

"No. I realized it was true, it wasn't real. I guess I was crazy. Am crazy."

"Everybody's a little crazy these days, Emily."

"Yes," said Emily, "I can see why folks would go to Las Vegas."

"Are you coming with me to New York?"

"I don't know, Bertie. If *it's* going to happen, this is the place I'd like to be. My parents would want me here."

"Sure, I can see that," Bertie said. His chest felt like he'd just swallowed a giant avocado pit.

"I believe that men and women . . ." Bertie started to say, but when he turned to Emily, she was staring at him with such big, open eyes that he couldn't remember what he was trying to say.

"What, Bertie?" Emily said dreamily, dreamily.

"We should be together," Bertie heard himself say, and clouds froze in the sky and birds stopped singing and the earth stopped breathing.

"I think so too," said Emily, and they kissed, and the world began again crashingly in Bertie's head. After some happy fumbling they found themselves in the embrace of love. The Kansas wheat field swallowed them up in waves of pulsating energy, and Bertie knew that he soared ever closer to the Book.

They agreed that she would not come right away, but would join him later if everything turned out all right.

Emily lay in his embrace. "I can't take all this happiness all at once, Bertie, love. Meeting you, seeing my parents, and being well again, it's all too much. I'm almost glad I'm going to stay here awhile. It will give me a chance to be with myself. You know how it is."

Bertie knew how it was, but that didn't stop his heart from luffing like a sail dead to the breeze. For him the afternoon had been like a moment in Paradise. Even the idea of separation was impossible.

"I understand," he said through gritted teeth, because in his mind he did understand, though his heart and his body sang the song of desire.

The next five days were ones of love and close companionship for Emily and Bertie. They were inseparable as they and the others prepared for the rest of the journey. Mr. Butterworth's foreman, like so many others, had quit his job, and when Mr. Sloat offered to take his place, the now over-worked farmer was happy to accept. Mrs. Sloat immediately began to plan a garden on the land surrounding the foreman's cottage. Now that Bertie's bunch numbered only seven, they could no longer masquerade as an association. Rufus pulled down the Santa signs, and Bertie cranked the front display from "Charter" to "Garage." Ben was also busy. He fashioned two bus mechanic uniforms from some old farmers overalls for himself and Rufus. If there was any trouble, Flora, Fawna, Del, and Bryce would hide in the back of the bus.

The bus was filled up with number-one diesel from Mr. Butterworth's private two-thousand-gallon tank, and off they went.

Emily stood at the end of the drive where the paved road began, her slim face glowing with new radiance. The morning sun was like a beacon pointing the way east. The state highway was arrow-straight. Bertie flipped down the sun visor. He and Emily exchanged last looks, then Bertie turned the bus onto the highway and drove toward the sunrise, toward New York.

Rufus went to the back of the bus to play "license plate" with Flora and Fawna. Del and Bryce smoked a joint and dreamed of the space ride they hoped was in their future. As Bertie shifted gears Ben, who was sitting near Bertie, read aloud a passage from *The New York Times*.

"'Still numbered among the many unexplained events at yesterday's Zoo Day fiasco is the mysterious presence and subsequent disappearance of the chimp's trainer, the so-called 'man in brown.' City officials say he is not a zoo employee, though the chimpanzee has been identified as being from the zoo's ape house. How the man managed to get hold of the chimp, in what way he created the illusion of speech, and where he is now are questions police are asking today.'"

15

The Tailor's Tale

After Ben finished reading the outdated newspaper article Bertie asked him, "If this 'man in brown' is Vith, and I think it is, and if he is the same one I was to see in the zoo, and I think he was, then why didn't he tell me who he was when I met him at the SPOM meeting?"

"He didn't know it was you, Bertie."

Bertie glanced toward Ben, wondering how the tailor knew that, but something caught his eye that made him forget all else. The tailor had his coat off, displaying the belt with the fairy-tale motto, but what startled Bertie was a small, fuzzy-looking tattoo on the tailor's inside right wrist. Bertie took a second quick glance to confirm his suspicion. The inked flesh was not an image but a row of numbers.

"You . . . you . . ." Bertie sputtered, "you were in a concentration camp?"

"Yes, Bertie."

"But that was fifty years ago. You couldn't have been more than ten years old!"

"True. Not even that."

Bertie didn't know what to say. He wanted to cry, and the

flat road ahead blurred in his filmy eyes, so he had to lean forward and blink hard and grip the wheel tight with both hands to control the bus.

"Oh, oh," sighed Bertie.

"What is it, my friend?" the tailor asked.

"I'm so sad, I'm so sorry," Bertie mumbled. He had never known anyone who had actually been a victim of that dark time, but he had always felt an overwhelming sorrow when he thought of their suffering.

"Do you want to talk about it?" Bertie asked, even though he was not at all sure he could bear to hear Ben's story.

"No, Bertie, I can't do that."

"Well, then, tell me about everything after the camps," Bertie said, relieved.

"I was hoping you'd ask," Ben replied. Then the tailor told his tale.

"When the camps were liberated, I was lucky enough to be one of the orphans the United States admitted..."

"Your parents were—I mean, they..."

"Bertie, please, nothing about the camps—and watch the road, will you? I was brought to America and I grew up in Brooklyn in a transplanted piece of the Warsaw ghetto. I spoke Yiddish. I learned the art of tailoring from an old man who had a shop on Flatbush Avenue where he sold clothing to the Hasidim. I was headed for a modest, ordinary life in New York when I had a dream that changed everything. You know how most dreams are remembered only in fragments, or dimly? This one I can recall in exact detail to this day. In it, one of the camp commandants, a man who had committed brutalities on members of my family, somehow had made it to America and set up a big factory. I went to him to ask him what he was doing, and he said, 'We're raising Jews for animal food, it's not fit for human consumption!' and he held up an unlabeled can shaped like a can of cat food.

"When I woke up, the seed of Revenge was planted in

my heart, and I had to find out if any of my captors had succeeded in escaping justice. Of course, many of them had done so, some with their stolen war booty, some with the aid of various foreign governments, including our own. I found out that the good old USA had aided and abetted some of those who had perpetrated crimes against humanity. I made it my mission in life to track them down and bring them to justice.

"At first I hunted them alone, found them out where they had set themselves up with new identities and administered justice myself. I admit I took pleasure in discovering them, growing as fat as their sheep or cattle on the Argentine pampas, or turning into superpatriotic Americans in their homes in Queens and Far Rockaway. The looks in their eyes when they realized their hour had come, that was what I lived for. Then, *zitzit*! a couple of rounds with a silencer. I never tortured them, as they had done to us, or starved them, or took away their pride until they were abject, submissive creatures.

"Then I met Vith—yes, Bertie, I am his emissary, sent to assure that you arrive safely. Think of me as your bodyguard. Come to think of it, Rufus fits the part more. Well, you have two now."

Bertie was speechless. He thought his psychic senses must be growing dull, since he hadn't picked up the vital signs of mystic involvement. He realized his love for Emily consumed his thoughts.

"You have nothing to say? Yes, Vith was a great influence on my life. He turned me away from my violent ways. He taught me a sweeter form of revenge, which is to let Justice, Karma, work its way. It was in Minnesota that I met him. I had found a certain Klaus Schmidt, a notorious camp guard, hiding as a Swiss immigrant in the lake country. He had a nice little dairy business and was growing old and obese in comfort. I was on my way to end his idyllic existence when my car gave out on the way to his farm.

"Imagine the scene, Bertie. Here I am miles from nowhere with my head stuck under the hood when I hear this voice say: 'You're doing it all wrong, you know.'

"I pop my head up so fast, I almost sprain my neck. 'What?' I say, thinking he's going to give me some advice on car repair.

"'Killing all those people,' he says. 'It's all wrong. You're not rectifying anything, and your own soul is in danger.'

"I look at him, bug-eyed. 'Who are you? Am I under arrest?'

"'Insofar as you are not moving, yes. My name is Vith Pankas and I'm here to help you.'

"'Where did you come from? I thought I was all alone out here,' I ask him, looking around for his car. There was no vehicle around other than my own.

"'I'm a traveler,' he says. 'I'm here to help you. You can't go on taking life if you expect to have a happy life yourself.'

"'I don't care about my life,' I said, and at the time it was true. 'I'm doing this for the dead.'

"'The dead are dead,' said Vith. 'Let them lie down. You are alive. It is you who must live now.'

"'They are alive too!' I shouted, meaning my former tormentors.

"'Ah, but when you kill them, you free them. You rush into it and you see only the trappings of a successful life when you find them. Shall we take Klaus Schmidt as an example? Let's go pay him a visit.'

"So we did. (My car started up as soon as we sat down in it.) We pretended to be milking-machine salesmen, and from somewhere Vith produced a shiny brochure describing the wonders of his milker, the Milky Way Milker. This pre-sense enabled us to spend a few minutes with Klaus. He and Vith discussed the merits of various farming techniques while I watched Klaus. I think Vith saw that I was skeptical, that I was still seeing only the happy Minnesota farmer. So, for an instant, just the barest fraction of a second, he showed me what it was like to be Klaus Schmidt. God, what a paranoid, depressed wreck of a man he was. He had brutalized his wife into a suicide. His children hated him because they knew his past, and the knowledge had ruined their lives also. Klaus had no friends. He trusted no one. He lived in fear of a visit from someone like me or the FBI or Immigration or inquiring reporters. And this fear was all-consuming. Even if his life had been free from other troubles, this constant anxiety wore him down. And he feared death. He longed to escape his life, yet the thought of divine judgment was horrifying.

As you might imagine, when we got back in the car, I was full of questions. Well, Bertie, you've had some experience with Vith. You know you don't get complete answers from him. He likes you to figure things out for yourself. But he always tells the truth, and most of the time it's just that we don't have the breadth of mind to understand what he tells us.

"I realized that what I was doing was avoiding my destiny. Klaus, and those like him, were no longer a danger. They had made their own fates, and I was wasting my energy hunting them down. There were other problems to be dealt with. Vigilance is necessary, but revenge is another thing altogether.

"Later Vith told me that I was to play a part in the final days of 'the world as you know it,' as Vith loves to put it. And that's why I was waiting by the side of the road for you. You're a very important person—did you know that, Bertie? Every policeman in the United States is looking for you, not to mention a few others who aren't agents of the law."

16

Reggie vs. Renstrom

Deep beneath the buffalo graveyard in Plains, Kansas, bunker mentality had set in like a layer of permafrost. When Starblaster Reggie shouted "We ready fo' 'em man, we ready— We got 'em targeted, yessir—We gonna blow their shit back where it came from—" Renstrom thought Reggie was trying to annoy him with his gung-ho slogans.

The struggle between the two cavemates had intensified. A small-scale guerrilla war was in progress. Renstrom had introduced some low-grade alpha-wave static into Reggie's stereo headphones, further disrupting Reggie's already jumbled circuitry. Reggie, for his part, had begun some subtle physical harassment, little things such as dominating the bathroom area with posters and hair dryers and towels, and wearing his pistol with the holster unsnapped.

World War III began with one of these incidents. Renstrom had programmed his console for a new electronic game he had invented himself. In a fit of pique he made the victim a black Afro-haired creature, which was chased through space by a monster that eventually, if the game was played correctly, caught it and ate it with appropriate screams and crunching sounds. Carl played the game for hours, his satisfaction growing every time the monster chomped the Reggie-image. Unfortunately for Renstrom, the aggressive alien looked exactly like Reggie's imagined enemy from another galaxy. One day Renstrom left the screen on and Reggie saw the image. Now he knew: Renstrom was an alien, in cahoots with Reggie's adversary. He must be destroyed.

Reggie had a unique plan. He would hunt Renstrom down with the Titan. It didn't matter if the target was right here in the silo. As long as Reggie had his Starshield on, he was invincible. He laid in an alternate targeting program.

17

Monkey

Monkey was a talking, magically endowed ape because Vith's ancestor had made him so. After his adventures in ancient China he had slept for thousands of years on the sleep known as Buddha's dream. Vith had summoned him back to the world of the six senses again. "When you are ready, you will assume your role of guardian, as you were in the old days."

"What, am I not Monkey the Terrible, the Fierce, the Bold Monkey?"

"You are a mistake, one of two my ancestor made. The other is Man."

Vith loved Monkey like a son. And Monkey was certainly prodigal. At first he was happy enough to follow Vith as the monochrome man went about his business, but soon he became naughty and mischievous again. As a prank, he showed off his talents to a group of businessmen, calling them silly fools to talk about potential profits when the world was about to be vaporized. (He was mimicking things he'd heard Vith say.) Instead of being shocked or indignant or surprised or scared, the businessmen actually had the temerity to leap on him and capture him. They took him to California, and kept

him hidden at Big Boys Camp, until _____ _____ began
his personal pursuit of Bertie.

Monkey sulked and fumed, confined in the second van of
the Accumulated Life vehicles. He was too weak to pry open
the bars of his cage. Most of his supernatural powers were
greatly diminished. He could no longer jump up to the clouds
in one leap, nor instantly change his form to any likeness,
nor cast a spell so the hairs on his head became hundreds of
little warrior monkeys, as in the days of his glory. But he
was still one tough old ape, as his captors found out when
they tried to torture him. Many years ago he had been dipped
in Lao Tzu's alchemical cauldron. No knife could cut him;
no brand could burn him; no blow could daunt him, nor even
dent him.

He was sure Vith was leaving him in captivity as punishment for running off, or perhaps for the wild story he'd told
at Big Boys Camp when Monkey placed himself at the center
of creation, aggrandized himself as a god, and gave the capitalists nightmares with the mishmash of gibberish he had
extemporized, ideas of Vith's distorted and exaggerated
through Monkey's playful consciousness.

Monkey decided to escape and find Bertie on his own. He
schemed and brooded in a corner. At last he hit upon an idea.

_____ _____ had located Bertie's hometown in Paradise and had decided to start his search there. His force was a
miniature rapid-deployment unit. _____ _____ drove the
first van; Monkey was being held in the second van; the third
van was a fuel truck, and the commando team had devised a
system for in-transit fueling. They made the trip from San Francisco to Paradise, Indiana in twenty hours.

It took only a few minutes for _____ _____'s advance scout to find someone who remembered "the old Rupp
place," even though it had changed hands four times in the
interim. The team set up a three-hundred-and-sixty-degree
stakeout with dreadful efficiency. Monkey made his move.

First he retired into meditation, summoning up all the power within him to make a single brief transformation. When he was sure he had the requisite energy for the feat, he asked to see _____ _____. The executive at first refused, but he came immediately when Monkey sent word of his offer: "My freedom for the secret of economical space travel."

"That's the problem for you, isn't it?" Monkey said as _____ _____ shut the van door. He had come alone, trusting no one to share what knowledge Monkey might impart. "You can take a dozen or twenty people with you, but you need room for thousands. Your solid-fuel boosters will never take you where you need to go. The answers are all in the Book."

"The Book, the Book. We can't understand it. Damn you. That Book is a curse. It's idiocy. Foolishness."

"To the foolish. But to the wise it is wisdom. There is one section of the Book specifically devoted to movement through space."

"Sure. The Book of Swoons. Garbage. I couldn't make anything of it."

"Yes, that's you. You have the Book, you have the Bible and the Koran and the Sutras, you have the secrets of the universe at your command, and still you don't understand.

"Remember what the Book says:

THE KINGDOM OF HEAVEN IS WITHIN YOU:
NO PRESERVATIVES ADDED:
TAKEN DAILY, PROVIDES FAST RELIEF."

The animal grinned, a wicked smile, but _____ _____ was not sensitive to the divine vibrations. He did not quiver with delight on hearing a few words from the mystical Book. Instead he spat on the outdoor carpet of the truck floor and cursed.

"See, that's what I mean. It's maddening."

"My freedom now for yours later."

"What do you know about rocket propulsion? No, we want to talk to the one who sent you. We don't want his philosophy, we want his technology."

"So you can carry on your plundering on other worlds? Vith won't like that."

"What can he do? We got you, didn't we?" _____ _____ was arrogant. "We'll get him, too, and if he won't tell us how to build the ship we need, we'll make him take us himself."

_____ _____, who had been pacing up and down in front of the cage, leaned his head back to give his short, brutal laugh. Monkey's long arm shot out and seized him around the throat. _____ _____ had forgotten the more-than-human strength and length of a monkey's limbs. Silently Monkey choked him while searching his pockets with one dexterous foot. He removed the keys with his toes and unlocked the cage, still throttling _____ _____.

Then he performed his transformation. In an instant there were two _____ _____s. Monkey threw his unconscious victim into the cell.

Before his enlightenment, he would have killed _____ _____, gleefully, but as a good Buddhist, Monkey could only kick the executive once or twice as retribution for his long imprisonment. Then Monkey stepped out of the van as _____ _____ and began to issue orders in a perfect imitation of _____ _____'s voice.

"No one is to enter this truck for the next twelve hours," he said, pointing to the one holding the cage. "I'm going to reconnoiter. You"—he waved at the driver of the first van— "drive. The rest of you wait here." With that he climbed into the cab.

Nearly a mile down the road the transformation weakened. The excited ape let out a great monkey whoop that nearly sent the startled driver into a ditch. He was an ex-Green Beret with combat medals, but by the time he reached for his holster, Monkey was on him. Monkey stripped the soldier and left him naked with a few obscene insults about his lack of body hair.

Now he was free, but how to proceed? Had he all his powers, he would have mounted a cloud chariot and called on the Dragon of the West Wind to pull him, or he'd have made a leap of one hundred thousand cubits and been there at once.

Like all monkeys, he was a supreme mimic and first tried to drive the van, but it careened all over the road and landed upside-down in a cornfield.

Dazed but unhurt, Monkey crawled from the wreckage, dusted the bits of cornstalk off his uniform, and began the walk to New York. After some distance he decided to try something he had seen others do. He stuck out his thumb, that marvelous, jointed, prehensile digit, and waved it at passing motorists. Sure enough, one soon stopped to pick him up. With his baseball cap, sunglasses, white jumpsuit with ACCUMULATED LIFE GROUP emblazoned on the back, and combat boots, Monkey resembled an extremely short and ugly teenager. Gloves and a windbreaker hood on the jumpsuit further disguised his apeness. The first person to pick him up was a drunk who barely glanced at him.

"Where ya goin', kid?"

"New York," said Monkey.

"Oh, yeah? I was there once. Right after the war. Say, where's your luggage?"

"I'm traveling light," said Monkey.

"I'll say you are. Hey, kid, did you see the excitement back up the road?" Monkey shook his head. "Some fool went clean crazy. Ran his van into a field, tore off all his clothes, and paraded up the highway bare-ass naked. When I went by, the cops had him, and they were trying to roll the van

back on its wheels. You didn't see that?" the driver asked.
He looked at his passenger through a drunken fog, with the
faintest glimmer of suspicion flickering on his face. Had this
kid run away from some kind of home or maybe a sideshow?

"I slept out last night. Actually I'm a dangerous criminal
who just escaped from prison." The man laughed. Monkey
did too. He was enjoying himself.

Sure, kid. Serving time in Joliet, huh? You and Al Capone.
Oh, yer a mean-looking mug, aren't you? That's some dis-
guise ya got on there, kid."

They bantered back and forth like this, each sure the other
was unaware of the humor of the situation, until the driver
got sleepy and asked if Monkey could drive for a while. He
was a traveling salesman going home to Youngstown from
Indiana, so Monkey would get all the way across Ohio if he
could keep the car on the road. While he and the inebriated
salesman were amusing each other with ridicule, Monkey had
been studying the operation of the vehicle with the same
intense concentration with which Bertie had observed bus
drivers.

"Sure, I can drive."

"Yeah, sure. I bet you're a regular grease monkey. Whoo!
Grease monkey, oh, that's a good one for you, sonny. Hey,
don't worry," the salesman said, concerned that he might
have gone too far, "you'll probably grow out of it." But inside
he thought "grease monkey" to himself and chortled again.
Monkey smiled his bared-teeth ape grin, though he would
have liked to have choked the fool.

The salesman lay down in the backseat and immediately
fell asleep. Monkey drove the car in a fine imitation of the
way the drunk salesman drove, accelerating and braking rag-
gedly, swerving erratically, and exceeding the speed limit by
fifteen or twenty miles an hour. He was almost to Youngstown
on the Ohio Turnpike before a trooper pulled him over.

"All right, you, out of the car." Monkey opened the door

and jumped to the ground. The salesman slumbered peacefully in the backseat. Monkey looked up into the mirrored sunglasses of the state policeman. Monkey was huge for his species. Wearing the heavy military boots, he was nearly five feet tall.

"What's with your friend?" the policeman asked him. Monkey raised his hand, thumb and fingers making a circle to his mouth. The trooper looked in the backseat, then at Monkey again. The thought flitted across the man's mind that the person in front of him looked incredibly like an ape, but that was impossible.

"All right, let's see your license." Monkey produced the wallet of a man now languishing in the county asylum in Paradise, trying to convince an exaggeratedly sympathetic doctor that a monkey really had stolen his clothes and his car.

As soon as he examined the document Monkey handed him, the state policeman instantly modified his behavior toward Monkey. He drew himself upright, saluted, and handed Monkey back his purloined credentials.

"Excuse me, sir. Is this your prisoner?" he said, nodding toward the prone figure in the rear seat. Monkey nodded sagaciously.

"He's not really drunk, he's sedated. We can't be too careful with one like him."

"I understand. Is there anything I can do for you?" the officer asked solicitously.

"Just make sure I'm not disturbed again."

"Yes, sir. Been on the road a long time, sir?"

"Why do you say that?" Monkey snapped.

"Well, sir, you were driving kind of funny, speeding up and slowing down."

"I'll try to keep a steady pace. What do you recommend?" said Monkey charitably.

"The speed limit is fifty-five, sir," the officer replied.

Behind Monkey's sunglasses the trooper could see two fiery red eyes (a monkey's eyes are naturally bloodshot), but his credentials were so impressive that the officer was compelled to accept them unquestioningly.

With siren screeching and lights rotating furiously, the trooper's car provided an escort to the state line for Monkey. At the border Monkey waved to the bewildered policeman. The trooper realized he had just confronted a monkey that spoke English and drove an automobile. Then the man's mind refused to acknowledge obvious facts. The thought paraded once rapidly across his consciousness, then was restrained by sawhorse sidewalk barricades of logic and reason. Like the salesman, he attributed Monkey's queer looks to extreme ugliness, possibly deformity.

Monkey congratulated himself again on his cleverness. Wasn't he the equal of men, even their better? Perhaps he would save the world, then they would make him their king, as he had been King of the Monkeys, before his escapades in Chinese Heaven. He woke up the salesman, who had slept through Ohio and the entire episode with the state trooper. Thanking him profusely, Monkey got out and stood at the side of the road. With a look of great joy on his face he extended his evolutionary link to his motorized brother, the toolmakers' necessity, in the universal sign for a free ride.

18

The Origin of Species (Revised Edition)

Bertie, Monkey and _____ _____ made their way east by separate routes. Bertie fretted. Monkey rejoiced in his new freedom. He pounced on every individual who picked him up. He demanded their life stories of them, then he told them fantastic tales of outer-space adventures with himself as the central heroic character. _____ _____ grimly pursued them both.

_____ _____ was a desperate man. Like Bertie, he had seen the inevitability of the holocaust. Unlike Bertie, he had not gone insane, but rather he had bent the whole of his considerable powers toward avoiding the conflict. Soon he realized that there was no safe place on Earth. No island was isolated enough, no arctic region remote enough, no mountain inaccessible enough, that the poisonous clouds of radiation would not contaminate it. He began to plan for emigration from the planet. When he saw he could not go on alone, he formed a consortium to raise the necessary funds. Big Boys Camps was a conference of participants.

The capture of Monkey had been an important piece

of luck. Contact with an alien culture could provide the information necessary to bring his plan to fulfillment. The subsequent escape of Monkey was a severe setback, but _____ _____ was a man of will and determination.

One night while Bertie and his group were having dinner at a Quaker meeting in Pennsylvania and Monkey was drinking Iron City beer and eating kielbasa sandwiches (shocking conduct for a Buddhist) with his latest ride at a roadside tavern outside of Pittsburgh, _____ _____ passed them both with his convoy of white insurance trucks. After the fiasco in Paradise, _____ _____ had set out at once for New York.

Although it had been almost two weeks since Zoo Day, the mood of the city was still on the ragged edge of awareness. The bird-shit crisis in the South Pacific was over, but the rumbling undercurrents of war were in crescendo. In a few weeks the general consciousness had swung from a kind of debauched fatalism into black depression. The voices of doom were heard everywhere, and yet *nothing* was done to lessen the tension between the would-be combatants. Leaders of both sides increased their belligerent posturing.

Against this backdrop, Zoo Day had been only a terrifying divertissement. _____ _____ infiltrated the zoo staff with ease. He learned that they knew nothing more than had been publicized about the stranger who was believed to have influenced their animals. Bertie Rupp would come here, of that _____ _____ was sure, and that foul ape, he'd show up, too, yes, and pay for his indiscretions, too, thought _____ _____. His troops staked out the area as only a military command can do, with infared sensors and thermal detection devices creating an artificial boundary around the zoo like a skin of exposed nerves.

Monkey ambled into town behind the wheel of a 1957 Thunderbird low-rider, recently refurbished by members of the Cool Salsa Gang of East Hoboken, New Jersey. They'd

picked up Monkey just off the Pulaski Skyway and taken him
the last few miles into New York. During the short ride he'd
convinced them he was just about the baddest dude around.
By the time they dropped him off at the zoo, he was a life
member of Cool Salsa.

He didn't bother about the CLOSED sign at the main entrance to the park. After burying his clothes Monkey climbed
up and over the fence into the zoo with ease. He found the
monkey house and entered it. There was some initial terri-
torial squabbling until the others understood that he was Monkey, the Legendary, their king. Once this was established, he
was content to have the other monkeys wait on him; they fed
him the choicest scraps, fanned him, and paid him homage,
until Vith's class that evening. Education had continued at
the zoo even after Zoo Day, though emphasis had shifted
from Voice and Articulation to Biology and Natural History.

Bertie stood on the cliffs of the Hudson River. New York
City lay across the dead body of water. (A recent major leak
at the nuclear power plant upriver at Bear Mountain had killed
every living organism in the river, in what should have been,
but was not, taken as a dire warning.) The bus was parked
several blocks away on a side street in Fort Lee. Bertie didn't
know what to do with it. Rufus wanted to jam the accelerator
pedal with a stick and send the Americruiser flying off a
precipice into the river, but Bertie said that would be littering.

On the tailor's advice they abandoned the bus and took
their possessions with them to a local bus terminal for the
short ride into the city. Sure enough, when they got to the
tollbooth, every long-distance bus with a big dog on it was
being halted and searched. The seven of them stuck closely
together and gained the anonymity that comes from being
perceived as a group.

Keeping closely linked, they repeated Bertie's subway ride
of his last visit. The Bronx had become even more charnel-

like. The smoke from smoldering fires amid the rubble cast a pall over the area. Hasty barricades had been thrown up at the intersection of border avenues, but whether they were to prevent entry by outsiders or to contain those within, Bertie could not tell.

As they approached the zoo Bertie grew apprehensive. Vividly unpleasant memories of his last visit cycled through his head. As they approached the main gate Bertie shuddered at the sight of men in white, patrolling the area with dogs. How was Bertie to find Vith? How could he let Vith know that he was here?

"Leave it to me," the tailor said. As the others watched from a distance he approached the guards. He had scarcely spoken a single low sentence to them when they grabbed him roughly and hauled him inside, the dogs barking furiously and nipping at his dragging heels.

Bertie burst into tears. Here he was so near to his goal, he thought, and yet he was helpless, and now his friend and protector was a prisoner. With his entourage in tow he walked away from the park into a small neighborhood of shops and delicatessens underneath the elevated trestle. In a coin-op Laundromat Bertie and Rufus washed the accumulated laundry from the trip while Del and Bryce did each other's charts and decided that today was a day of great "potential."

While the clothes were spinning in the dryer Bertie called Roscoe. He remembered his friend's warning, but he was getting desperate.

"I can't talk to you from here," Roscoe hissed when he realized it was Bertie. "Call me back in three minutes at this number. Tell me where you are, then hang up right away." Roscoe gave Bertie the number, and Bertie did as he was told. In this way Roscoe was able to join the despondent group at the Laundromat.

"A mime. Far out," Del mumbled. He and Bryce had chosen this evening to take the special mushrooms they'd been saving ever since California. Bryce was curled up in a corner with Flora and Fawna, who were reading to her from a children's book of European fairy tales Ben had given them.

"'Rapunzel, Rapunzel, let down your hair!'" read Flora.

"Oh, wow!" said Bryce, fingering the blond ringlets on her own head.

"'Then Rapunzel let down her hair and the Prince climbed up,'" Fauna continued.

Bertie and Roscoe held a somber reunion.

"I've decided to go in after him," said Bertie, his resolve now glistening like the fresh skin of a molted snake. "He'd do the same for me, and besides, I just know Vith is in there."

"How are you going to get over the wall?" Roscoe asked, always practical, as a mime must be to solve the puzzle of movement in the invisible world.

"I'm going to stand on Rufus's back."

"That won't get you over, but a three-man pyramid might. I'll go. I've got the perfect outfit for the job, anyway." Roscoe gestured to his habitually black attire.

Darkness fell over the Bronx. Like the African jungle, it took on a menacing aspect in the nighttime, a sense that strange and powerful predators lurked unseen. Bertie reasoned that it was best for them all to remain together, so Rufus carried a sleepy pair of sisters, and the unsteady psychedelisized couple supported each other with waves of giggles until Roscoe pantomimed them into silence.

They picked a spot fifty yards or so from the main gate, behind some shrubbery.

Just as Rufus was about to brace himself against the wall, an action that certainly would have breached the delicate sensory field of _____ _____'s paramilitary unit, Flora gave out a little shriek. The gates of the zoo swung open silently, and from within came a ghastly, otherworldly glow and swirling, gentle, eerie music. Like Jesus and Buddha,

Vith tried to tailor his presentations to suit the mental makeup of his audience.

Bertie led his people in through the entrance. Ahead in the same clearing where the Zoo Day festivities had taken place, Vith hovered on a cloud-throne a few feet off the ground. The tailor stood beneath and to the right of him, beaming broadly. His assignment was completed. _____ _____ and his men had come running when the strange light and sound show began, but they were not about to attack the spectacle of Vith. They stood awed and transfixed, as did Bertie and those with him, while Vith spoke.

"Welcome Bertram, welcome everyone. There is no need for guns or violence, for the words I speak are free to all. Monkey, you rascal, come out of that cage and show yourself. Someone find Miss Cheetah; this is a special evening and she should be here." _____ _____, though intensely absorbed in the scene, issued the necessary orders, and Cheetah soon joined them.

"Tonight, class, we have a special honored guest, another pupil of mine, the earnest and hardworking devotee, Bertram Rupp." The animals showed their respect with a bewildering array of sounds that conveyed their admiration. "Also in attendance tonight is a man—some of you may have seen him skulking about during the past two days—who is one of the corrupters, the polluters, the defilers. In his trophy room are the mounted heads of elk, rhino, bear, and moose—" Vith was interrupted by a savage din as the animals expressed their displeasure in no uncertain terms.

"Nonetheless, he is as welcome as Bertram to sit in on our class tonight. Why is that? Because, as I have said, the truth is an open book."

"Mister!" Flora squeaked.

"What is it, my child?" Vith asked.

"We wanna ride up there," said Fawna, completely unafraid.

"If you promise to be quiet while I talk." The two little girls nodded their heads vigorously. Vith wafted them up onto his airy seat.

"Now, class, where were we? Oh, Monkey, you wicked thing, there you are." For the second time in his life Bertie saw the extraordinary Monkey. The reckless ape stood under Vith and shook a hairy fist upward. He would have thrown one of his terrible tantrums, but Vith superseded him with a command.

"Class is now in session. Who can tell me where I left off?"

"Darwin!" came a call from the elephants' pen.

"Quite right. Darwin. Tonight, my friends, I shall address the human audience, but be aware, humans, my zoo class understands every word. When Charles Darwin issued his landmark opus of biological ordering and classification, *The Origin of Species*, he was working with the best information available to him at the time. He collected many of the facts himself on his many expeditions to remote islands in search of unusual flora and fauna. Though he understood the principles of nature correctly, he failed to identify the one flaw in his well-constructed pyramid of evolution: man.

"Genus, family, order, class, phylum. Protozoan, sponge, flatworm, insect, crustacean, vertebrate, amphibian, reptile, bird, mammal. How neatly, beautifully, and logically it all fits together, except for man. Even the wildest, most bizarre creations in nature can be explained: the neck of the giraffe, the peacock's feathers, the oddity of the duckbill platypus. Each variation grew out of causes and conditions for adaption of the creature to its circumstances. But man is not the product of billions of years of natural evolution. He is an anomaly, a freak, the result of unnatural tampering by outside influences. I am referring to the visit, some thousands of years ago, of beings from my home, so many many light-years distant.

"It's time that I reveal for you everything that has been clouded in the fog of myth and rumor. Many of your earliest legends are based on the deeds of our landing party. It was us who provided the spark that lit your minds and alienated you from your animal ancestry. What a mistake! What a poor choice! What a foolish, reckless, destructive act that was.

"Your species was not prepared to enter the rigorous self-discipline required by sentient beings. Instead you became the dominant hunters of your planet. Instead of joining the universal community of spirit, you used our gift to become merely more successful animals.

"We should have known that this was going to happen, and of course, the psychic giftwaves should never have been bequeathed. Yet at the time the temptation was overwhelming. On a journey through your galaxy we wandered through this Paradise. We marveled at the fantastic complexity of lower life-forms here. We saw a few dirty, slouching man-creatures. For us it was like looking at our past, for we, too, had risen out of primordial slime in the long, leisurely course of our own evolvement. A member of our party decided to play at being a god. Although it was strictly forbidden, he whispered certain secrets in the ear of the most intelligent specimens he could find. That's right. The snake in the story of Adam and Eve—he was one of my forebears. It took no more than the transmission of a few simple facts. The whole of science builds itself on comprehension of a handful of principles. When a tribe understands that heat releases energy, it is not long before that tribe can produce the heat necessary to split atoms.

"The rest of your world's history is tainted by this ill-advised intrusion. Who knows what kind of beings might have evolved in the natural course of things if we hadn't interfered. To thrust such advanced knowledge onto a primitive species, well, you've had the opportunity to see the scene played out again whenever twentieth-century culture encountered aboriginal society, as happened in Papua, New Guinea, and elsewhere. The resulting shock is devastating to the integrity of the less developed structure. Have I made myself clear? It's not entirely your fault, this disastrous state of affairs. Knowledge is man's crown of distinction. It is also his crown of thorns.

"Consider the ants. Before man existed, before any of the mammalian order had evolved, ants were well established in their complex patterns of existence. What is their concept of time, these creatures who attain a kind of eternal life by being mere cells in the ongoing organism of the colony?

"The leaf-cutters build elaborate mounds of tunnels and chambers, sometimes a city block in size. The army ants have marched incessantly through the African jungle for millions of years, nightly making themselves into living structures to house their queen, in the same manner that they link themselves together in ant bridges to traverse gaps in their path. What fantastic energy and purpose at work there!

"A word from us and they—not you—might have been the rulers of this world. Instead, recklessly, and, I repeat, completely against a billion-year tradition of ethical behavior, the natural order was altered. I fully believe that it was this one unwarranted act that has led to your present critical condition. Are there any questions?"

"What about space travel?" asked _____ _____, who, though enthralled with the lecture, had not forgotten his original purpose.

"Yes?"

"How do you accomplish it?"

"Your scientists have only recently begun to suspect what others have known for thousands and millions of years: that the components of space, time, and matter are mere manifestations of the One. When you understand this, you can go anywhere, anytime."

"But how?"

"It will take you many incarnations to find out." Vith's simple statement was intended as a rebuke and taken by _____ _____ as such. His arrogance swelled up.

"I'll know now!" he shouted.

"I've already told you; you didn't hear me. Enough!" Vith raised a hand. The sourceless light illuminating the area dimmed to a pale pink-and-blue glow. A peculiarity in the atmosphere of Vith's planet refracted all light into brown, Vith's color; consequently he loved to play with the rainbow palette of light potential on Earth. Also, he had discovered that changes in light created radical alterations in the mood of those within its aura. Always the dramatist, Vith lowered himself to just above the heads of his audience.

"The time has come," he said quietly. "Bertram, collect your people together and please accept Monkey as your newest protector. Now you have three, as you should."

"What do you mean, Vith, 'the time has come'?" Bertie asked.

"You know."

Bertie's knees turned to water. His eyes crossed and wandered in their orbs. He sat down, right where he was. "You mean . . . ?" Bertie left the obvious question unstated.

Vith nodded silently in return.

"There isn't any hope? What about the Book?"

"Ah, Bertram. The Book is Eternal. You must keep searching for it."

"But, but—he has it!" Bertie cried, pointing to _____ _____, whose men had unobtrusively surrounded the others.

"Yes, and I'll keep it too, and I'll keep you," _____ _____ said, pointing at Vith, who smiled from his cloud-throne as the two little girls waved down to Rufus and made faces, "until you tell me what I need to know."

"Too late." Vith's voice rang with authority.

"But what about the children, all the children!" Bertie shouted.

"I'm sorry, Bertram, but I cannot stop the thing from happening."

"What about Emily?" cried Bertie in a sudden panic, but his voice was overwhelmed by other voices.

"What about us?" The call rose up from the surrounding cages. "Don't leave us to die in here. Give us our chance, Vith Pankas."

There was a soft chiming sound that reminded Bertie of Tinkerbell in Peter Pan; then the cages opened of themselves. After a moment of anticipatory silence, pandemonium erupted. The animals, under Vith's direction, encircled the surprised soldiers, who themselves were surrounding Bertie's group. The enraged beasts then broke through _____ _____'s inner circle. With an escort of elephants and big cats Bertie led his people out of the zoo. He didn't see the exact instant when Vith disappeared, but then, the essence of magic is distraction.

19

Sanctuary

Bertie's entourage now consisted of a mime, a tailor, an unemployed security guard, two little girls, a spaced-out couple, a monkey, and a chimpanzee. The tailor seemed to know what he was doing, as he directed Bertie to the ALG vans. They took the largest van, the Super Carryall. Bertie steered out onto the street (it seemed natural for him to be the driver), dodging an occasional rhino on White Plains Avenue. The zoo animals, as Vith had predicted, were not well suited for freedom in the city. Many were hit by automobiles, others were gunned down (those that had the misfortune to enter certain areas were killed and eaten). A few managed to flee north out of the city and lived their last few days in the wilds of Yonkers.

Once he got away from the scene, Bertie turned to the tailor and asked, "Where are we going?"

"Vith has chosen a place. I'll take you there." The tailor was cryptic.

"I need a bigger van. I need a bus," Bertie said in an insistent tone.

"What for, there's only a few of us?" the tailor asked in

surprise, but Bertie was unrelenting. At last the tailor agreed to Bertie's demand. Bertie changed into his bus driver's costume, strolled into Port Authority, and stole another bus with a boldness that astonished even himself.

Then the party discovered why Bertie wanted a bus. In the next hour before he left New York City, Bertie kidnapped eighty-nine children between the ages of three and seven. When they crossed the George Washington Bridge heading west on Route 80, the inside of the bus was a riot scene.

Only an inspired performance by Roscoe saved Bertie's desperate rescue effort from turning into a fiasco. Many of the children didn't want to be in the crowded, hot, uncomfortable machine.

Roscoe danced in the narrow aisle. He sang. He made puppets. He led the children through their initial fear of Monkey and Cheetah. Monkey remained aloof, but Cheetah soon became the children's favorite. All the while Bertie took them farther and farther from the homes and families they would never see again.

Bertie had no problem justifying his radical and drastic actions. It was all he could do, it was random, impartial, it was a blind act of compassion. He couldn't understand why a man, or rather, a being, of Vith's immense powers could not stop the insanity, but since Vith couldn't save them all, Bertie would do what he could. A few children would be saved.

Bertie stopped several times and frantically dialed Kansas, but no one answered at the Butterworth residence. By midnight they were many miles from New York. Bertie got very tired, and at last he relinquished the wheel to Ben, not without a small protest from Monkey, who wanted to try his hand at the big machine. Ben proved to be a proficient bus driver, so Bertie, exhausted by the shock of what Vith had told him, quickly fell asleep.

Rufus, who already had his hands full with Flora and

Fawna, did what he could to help with the new arrivals. Del and Bryce retreated to the last seat of the bus. Nothing could touch them, as they were in the raptures of bliss. The hallucinatory vision of Vith on his majestic cloud had permanently dislocated portions of their brains.

Late in the night the bus turned off Route 80 and began a winding journey through the narrow back roads of the Pocono Mountains. For many miles Ben steered the huge ten-wheeled vehicle through the darkness. The first light of dawn was glinting off the lake when Ben pulled the bus up to the front porch of a lodge that was an Eastern version of the one at Big Boys Camp. The forest was filled with Eastern conifers instead of redwoods, and the lake had a mucky, mulchy bottom instead of the smooth pebbles and imported sand at Big Boys Camp, but otherwise it was very similar. Vith stood on the porch with his hands hidden in the pockets of his brown jacket. Out of the bus stepped Bertie, rubbing his eyes from sleep.

"Hello, Vith."

"Hello, Bertram."

"Where are we?" Bertie asked.

"A secret place. A place of refuge. Here you will be safe until the danger is over."

"Oh, no!" said Bertie, "I can't stay. There's so many other people I have to tell." Vith shook his head slowly, once. He was about to lecture Bertie on the principle of the karmic wheel when the tailor appeared behind Bertie, then the children started pouring out of the bus. Vith's eyes widened a little, and he came near to disturbing his perfectly quiescent mind. It was an odd assortment of white, brown, red, and yellow bodies in various styles of dress and states of dishevelment.

"Bertram, you've outdone yourself." Bertie smiled sheepishly. "From now on, however, you must remain here. I cannot guarantee your safety should you leave."

Despite this warning, Bertie made expeditions to the nearest large cities over the next three days, kidnapping another ninety-four children. When Vith saw the growth in the population of diminutive refugees, he only smiled and stepped up his output of the miracle of the fishes and the loaves. Despite repeated phone calls to Kansas, Bertie was unable to contact Emily or her family.

On the morning of the fourth day at camp, as Bertie prepared for another "kid run," Vith came up behind him and put a hand on his shoulder.

"Not today, Bertram." Bertie turned to look at Vith. The Great Compassionate One transmitted his sadness through his hand into Bertie's body. Bertie's face turned pale. "Why don't you ask Roscoe to take the children for a walk?"

20

The Way the
World Ends

One fine September day in the late 1980s, Reggie Wilson activated his new Renstrom−sensitive targeting program. Carl Renstrom thus became the first individual human in history to be hunted with a nuclear bomb.

There was madness in Reggie's method. First he simulated an all-out enemy missile launch. In the sealed bunker, with no outside sources of information to confirm the event or contradict its reality, Carl Renstrom was convinced by Reggie's ploy. He was certain that his country was under attack, and he willingly executed his duties, for the launching of a nuclear missile requires the cooperation of both fire-control duty officers. He was unaware that ironically he was lending a hand in his own execution.

Reggie was quietly, insanely confident that his imaginary Starshield would protect him from the effects of the blast. He whooped with joy as the silo trembled from the reverberating rocket exhaust.

By the time the base commander realized that there was something terribly wrong in Silo 5, it was too late. The

Renstrom—seeking missile soared, reversed itself, and plunged toward the smoking hole from which it had emerged.

Ten miles down the road at the Butterworth farm, Emily had time to glance up in terror from the letter she was writing to Bertie. In the fields Mr. and Mrs. Butterworth were walking hand in hand amid their beloved wheat, their hearts full of joy because their daughter was a daughter again. The elderly couple had their backs to the blast. They entered eternity together and at peace.

Reggie Wilson's atomic annihilation of Renstrom was the explosion necessary to trigger the larger cataclysm, the way a hydrogen bomb is detonated by using a small atomic bomb for a blasting cap.

When the enemy saw an intercontinental ballistic missile bursting into flight, or rather when satellite sensors detected the incident and relayed its statistical existence to the enemy's main defensive computer, it logically determined that an attack had been initiated. Therefore it ordered the massive "launch on warning" that had become the foundation of both sides' defensive strategy. Confronted with thousands of incoming nuclear missiles, the American command responded with their full armament. The full-scale holocaust had been set in motion, irrevocably and uncontrollably.

21

What the
Missile Felt

I have poised here for two years, ninety-seven days, four hours, and twenty-three seconds, since my installation by Chief Engineer Valerie Vissarionovich Suslov. Ever alert, ever watchful, I have waited in darkness while the powers readied themselves for my use.

I know exactly what to expect. The initiation phase has begun, please wait. In six seconds the metal covering above me will draw back, yes, there is the sky, first light. This trip will take twenty-nine minutes and two seconds. Throughout my long, sleek body systems are humming to life, and at my base the powerful main thrust engines are staged for explosion. I rise in thundering majesty out of the Siberian plain, executing a roll maneuver of one half revolution to the right in the first hundred feet. The thick atmosphere rubs invisibly along my surface. I heat and glow, but my titanium skin is impervious. Soon I burst into the immensity of space. I revel in the lightness, the coolness, the deep darkness of it. I travel at five, six, ten times the speed of sound, yet I could be floating—such is the sensation—except that my booster engines are on and the auto gyro calculates my forward motion and rate of descent, for I am already plummeting back toward Earth. The trip is so brief. I would have gone on forever, a harmless speck of metal in the great Void of Space, but that is not my mission. I am programmed to perform a series of reverse thrusts to pitch me into the reentry mode. Now the heat comes again, much more intense than before, but I can withstand it. In the last seconds I break through some high cloud cover and I have time to see the sun rising over San Francisco Bay before everything disappears in a brilliant flash of white light.

22

The Circus After
World War III

"We were with the children, like children, at summer camp. We were just clowns. We didn't do this awful thing." Roscoe was insane.

"I know that. It's all right. Relax." The captain tried to quiet him.

"I didn't do it. I had nothing to do with it. I'm a clown."

His face was clownlike. It was a Modigliani face, long and thin and somber, with enormous, sad eyes that inquired about and accused all they saw. Roscoe's face was a child's face, of the kind a child trusted immediately and implicitly.

"I didn't do it. But don't ask them. Ask yourself. I'm innocent."

The captain shrugged. He couldn't ask himself. He feared the answer he might get. He wore the uniform Roscoe hated. Roscoe, an artist, who in better times would have been discriminating and perceptive, was blindly, bitterly, aggressively resentful of anything military. He knew that the man was a doctor, but all that Roscoe saw was the uniform.

Roscoe spoke again. "The day it happened, the air over

the Poconos was still and clear. We all climbed the nearest hill, the whole camp, we did a lot of things all together like that. Today was going to be my day.

"I was the leader running the camp. Today I was going to demonstrate hiking by compass. Oh, I thought I was so smart. We went up a nearby hill. It was bald and flat and higher than everything else, so that it seemed like the top of the world. I had them form into groups, according to where they were from, and lined them up on the points of the compass: to the east, New York; to the southeast, New Jersey; to the south, Philadelphia; west toward Pittsburgh; and north, Scranton and Wilkes-Barre.

"I indicated where each city was over the horizon. The kids stared excitedly, straining, as though if they looked hard, they'd see their homes. Seconds later there were explosions at every place I'd pointed. Not mushroom clouds—we were too far away to see them—but fantastic flashes of light. Then the sky glowed blackly. One missile passed above our heads in a smooth arc from beyond the North Pole. We saw it as a flame, not a shape. It dipped over the edge of Earth and blew up Bethlehem, probably aimed for the steel mill there, with my kids from Bethlehem and Allentown watching."

"It took out the nuclear research lab at Lehigh, top-secret, but I think I can tell you, since it's gone now." (The officer's interjection was intended to make Roscoe feel better, but it sent him off on a new tangent.)

"Serves them right. At least they killed each other."

"They had a name for it: Retaliation on Leadership Apparatus." (Once again the captain doctor tried to cheer him up.)

"The kids thought I did it, I called it down from heaven. I gestured, and it was all blown up, blown away. Some of them knew it was a nuclear war; most of them knew it. The rest were just scared. They were scared like animals before a flood or a fire. They knew to be afraid.

"But they didn't go numb. First they cried and screamed. Later, during the electrical storms—God, they were fierce, monumental, like the weather on Mars or Venus. We didn't expect them; I'd never read about them, nor the floods and earthquakes that followed.

"We all stayed in the camp dining hall. The storms went on. The sky grew black from the fires, and it was the darkness and noise that put the kids away. They couldn't sleep, and they couldn't crawl under the beds, not all of them, so they withdrew. They wouldn't eat, they wouldn't talk. They wouldn't look at me.

"At first I was frantic to care for them. But it was hopeless. They wouldn't respond."

Outside, the black sky crackled and discharged in unnatural frenzy. The interrogator shut off the recorder.

"Christ," he said, "we might get caught in a forest fire up here."

"I'll take it over the fire storm." The clown was succinct.

The soldier sent him away. He couldn't take it anymore, that long face staring at him with reproving eyes.

23

The Roll Call
of the Dead

When the captain first spotted the anomaly of life in the irradiated atmosphere of the Poconos, he ordered his helicopter, a huge troop carrier, to land on the lakeshore. He and his crew had been ordered into the air at the first alert, and their task was to search for survivors. He interviewed Roscoe, who then vanished. He looked to the care of the children. They seemed remarkably well-fed, although psychologically traumatized. He made futile attempts to find out why this tiny portion had been spared in the otherwise poisoned or obliterated northeast. No natural phenomena would seem to account for it, nor did these people seem capable of contriving any device that might have saved them. The counselors struck the captain as odd; none of them, except the mime, seemed to have the kinds of skills one would normally associate with running a camp program. After listening to them, the captain decided he was probably dealing with a religious group of some kind. This was undoubtedly their summer camp, he thought to himself, though it was hard to understand what kind of group would have such a mixture of nationalities.

Later the Army captain who had interviewed Roscoe found the mime's body, in the full lotus position, relaxed, smiling, and stone cold.

Many like Roscoe had gone off by themselves to die, even among the military; those who wanted to join others and those who couldn't face the future, such as it was going to be.

When the captain was ready to leave, the helicopter died and he and his troops were stuck in the camp. There was at least one very disturbing thing about this camp—the two talking monkeys. His men pointed out to him that actually they were a monkey and a chimpanzee, but since a talking animal was impossible, the distinction seemed pointless. No one else in this crazy setup seemed to find it strange when the animals spoke. They simply replied. Even the children were at ease with them.

For seven weeks the Army captain remained in his un-chosen seclusion drafting reports, which sometimes mentioned the monkeys and sometimes did not. Radio communication was impossible. He knew his superiors would assume that he and his men had died in a helicopter crash or from the effects of the deadly, lingering poison wind that contaminated bombed areas. To pass the time the officer tried to figure out why this sector was untouched, or rather, what shield or field existed around the boundaries of the camp to a distance of exactly six hundred meters in all directions before the Geiger counters and radiation detectors of his troops went from inactive to readings off the high end of the scale, but he was never able to clear up the mystery. And where did all the food come from?

Meanwhile Bertie grieved. Bertie had set out to read the Tibetan Book of the Dead for the whole world. Even though some small portions of the planet had escaped destruction, the long-term effects of the event had yet to show themselves.

For a man whose worst fears had just been realized, Bertie was in remarkably good spirits. His neurosis, the nucleomitophobic dread, had been confronted, and Bertie had survived. He spent the next two months in self-mortification and fasting, allowing his body to fester and sore while eating only a soup of boiled nettles and water. He read incessantly from the funerary verses of the Bardo Thodol, the Egyptian Book of the Dead, passages from the Bible, and the Jewish litany known as the Roll Call of the Dead. He had moved into a hut in the hills above camp the day the military arrived and passed this period of mourning there. When Rufus visited him, he persuaded his friend to leave him in solitude.

He built an altar of stones and branches where he prayed and raved and wept alone.

"'O nobly born, thy present intellect, in real nature void, is the very reality, the All-Good, the Immutable Light, the Clear light.'"* Thus he would recite during the day, but at night when strangely wild electrical storms pummeled the camp, he would bare his chest and call on the heavens to strike him down. Wailing and lamenting his misery for the world, for himself, for Emily, for all those people whose modest and decent lives deserved a better fate, Bertie undertook the rigors of extreme asceticism.

With only the bitter broth to fortify him, Bertie roamed the countryside within the limits established by Vith. He abandoned those children he had so courageously and compassionately plucked to safety, while he wrestled with the root question of his existence.

"'O this is now the hour of death. By taking advantage of this death, I will so act, for the good of all sentient beings, peopling the illimitable expanse of the heavens, as to obtain the Perfect Buddhahood, by resolving on love and compassion toward the Sole Perfection,'"† Bertie chanted.

*Tibetan Book of the Dead, Part 1, translated by W. Y. Evans-Wentz.

†Ibid.

" 'For dust thou art, and to dust thou have returned,' " he then chanted paraphrasing the Bible, and he thought of Emily, her dust mingled with the corrupted dust of the Kansas plain where nothing would grow for a thousand years, and off he would go into the forest, uttering inhuman cries as he thrashed through the underbrush, oblivious to the lacerations of prickers and thorns.

This phase lasted for the duration of the reading of the Bardo, a total of forty-nine days.

When he emerged from this intensely lugubrious time, Bertie was possessed of a new confidence in himself and his destiny. Rufus, who visited him from time to time to try to force food on him, noticed the change immediately. Bertie stumbled back into camp like a sickly ghost.

"You a diff'unt fella, Bertie. How you been, man?"

"I'm better, Rufus. How are the kids?"

"They all right. Childrens' strong. Know what I mean?"

"Uh-huh, I do," said Bertie. His skin was a moldy green color from lack of nutrition. "Is the Army still here?"

"They is. They can't leave. They stuck here with us."

"What happened?" Bertie asked.

"Nuthin'. They helicopter won't take off. Most likely be that Vith again, if'n you aks me."

Bertie managed a laugh. "You're probably right, Rufus."

"I liked it better when we was travelin', Bertie."

"Even on the bus, Rufus?"

"Even den. I likes city life, not this laid-back country stuff."

"There aren't any cities anymore, Rufus. Not in our country."

"I can't believe it. I wish I could see for myself."

"Me too. Vith could take us there," said Bertie.

"He gone too," Rufus replied.

"When?"

"Hard to say. You know him, how he be. Here one minute,

gone de nex'.'" Rufus chuckled. "'Bout two weeks ago I noticed he wer'n't around no mo'. Lef' a big pile of food behint, dough."

"Did he say anything before he left—about me, I mean?" Bertie asked.

"He did. He said"—and here Rufus drew himself up, although Vith was half a foot shorter than even a slouching Rufus, and did his best impression of the alien—"he said, 'Tell Bertram to keep searching.'"

"That's all?"

"That's it, boss. An' he tol' the three of us, Monkey, Ben, an' me, to keep an eye on you. We a team."

"I guess I should talk to that Army man now," said Bertie. His feelings toward the military mirrored Roscoe's, for whom Bertie had said a special mantra many thousands of times during his isolation.

The officer was very eager to question him; when the emaciated Bertie appeared at his tent, he launched impatiently into the interrogation, ignoring even the most basic formalities.

"Look, Rupp, I've been here seven weeks. I've got to get back, let my colonel know I'm alive, I haven't lost my command. You understand?"

"The Army is going to rule things now? Is that it? Haven't you done enough already?"

"Rupp, listen, I feel as bad as you. Okay, I haven't gone out and made a mess of myself in the forest like you, but I've grieved. I lost everybody, wife, kids, parents, friends. You notice I'm not wearing a gun? None of my men are, either."

"Did you meet Vith?" Bertie asked suddenly.

"Yes, we did."

"Did he . . . instruct you?" Bertie questioned his supposed interrogator.

"Yes, and what a remarkable man. You know, Bert—may

I call you Bert? I was a psychologist in private life; never in my association with any other practitioner did I meet a man so in tune with the feelings of others. It was as if he could read my mind." Bertie could imagine Vith conforming his presentation to the military man with the doctorate in psychology.

"Was it he who convinced you to give up your arms?"

"Yes, Bert. What do you know about him? Where is he now? I'd like to talk to him some more; so would my men. They—we—want to know what to do now."

"Vith won't tell you that. He'll tell you to find out for yourself. What would happen if you went back to your base and told your commander you were giving up your guns for peace?"

"I'd be court-martialed."

"Yes. So maybe you're better off that your helicopter's not working."

"Who told you about that?" the military man barked in surprise.

"My friend Rufus."

"Yeah, that gets me around to the subject of your group. Even though we're renouncing our weapons, we've got to remain the authorities here, as representatives of the government. Now everybody we talk to says you're the leader. Just what is your relationship with this Vith and why are you here?"

"The truth?"

"Please."

"Vith warned us the war was coming. Ben, the tailor—"

"What's his connection?"

"I guess you could say he's another one of Vith's converts. He led us to this spot. We were here when . . . when it happened."

"I see." The psychologist scratched at his newly grown beard. "I'm going to put my confidence in you, Bert. Did you know that everything outside the limits of this camp is a wasteland for many hundreds of miles?"

"Yes, I figured as much."

"How can that be? How can that be?"

"Did you ask Vith?"

"No. I forgot. He did most of the talking, anyway. Bert, you're a religious man of some sort. Do you know the line 'God works in mysterious ways, his wonders to perform'?"

"Yes, I know it," Bertie replied.

"I think this is divine intervention. I think Vith is God," the captain whispered dramatically.

"No!" said Bertie firmly. "Not God, not a god. A being, like ourselves. We should all be like him." Suddenly Bertie felt very faint. The officer called for assistance. Two soldiers escorted Bertie to the cabin where the tailor and Rufus had taken up residence. His two human guardians laid him on a prepared bed. Slightly delirious, Bertie managed a few words before he drifted off to sleep.

"Okay, I'm all right. I'm better than okay. I'm good. I survived. We survived. What can happen to us now?"

24

Cetacean Heaven

Great changes were occurring in the ocean depths. Both polar ice caps were melting from the intense heat of nuclear explosions and from the general warming trend of weather patterns altered by the holocaust. As the ice caps dissolved into the seawater around them, the temperature level in the oceans dropped. The radical difference in air and water temperature created new and more furious storms, which increased the melting of the caps, and this drove the temperature down further, sending the unstable weather systems into new frenzies; a vicious cycle of warming air and cooling water fed on itself until the storm was so violent that the whales and other sea mammals were afraid to surface for their air. They stayed submerged to the limits of their endurance.

A meeting of whales was held off the North Atlantic coast. Around and around swam the Greenland right whales, forty and fifty tons apiece, dwarfing their pygmy relations. Blues and grays and sperm whales sent delegations from their waters far away.

"The ships are gone! Their harpoon guns are no more. We

are rid of the curse of man. Rejoice!" sang the humpback whales in the intricate, never-ending song of their lives.

"Cold! We're cold!" moaned others. Many of the ocean creatures had died already. The warm-blooded mammals were coping better than their marine co-dwellers, but none knew how long and at what intensity the crisis would continue. A late-arriving humpback brought news: "Word has come of one from the province of the land dwellers who might be able to help us. He is said to speak the universal language of brotherhood."

The gathering decided to send a delegate in search of the Samaritan who was reported to have freed many animals from prison just before the catastrophe. A female rorqual was chosen as representative, not only because she was a fast swimmer but also because her family had been one of the most persecuted by man.

There was no need for a formal message. Theirs was the last desperate plea of a dying race. For a day and a night the graceful rorqual swam down the coast of North America, approaching cautiously the formerly dangerous coastline where boats of men once crowded the shore waters. Now there were no boats—nor man, either—but some special sense told the whale that further approach to the ruined earth would be harmful. At Montauk Point off the tip of Long Island she sounded, imitating the behavior of her cousin the humpback with prodigious leaps out of the water, smacking her flippers on the surface with resounding slaps that could be heard for miles and tossing up volumes of white water as she crashed back under. Then she paraded up and down a short section of coast, blowing up spumes of steamy air and mucus, calling attention to herself in every way she knew.

At last Vith appeared, riding a little wave that broke nicely under him as it smoothly carried him forward. When he approached the rorqual, he got off the wave and sat down on the water before her.

"Hello," he said.

"Greetings from the warmbloods of the sea." The rorqual made a gesture with her broad, flat tailfin, which was the whale equivalent of a curtsy.

"Ah, yes," said Vith, "tree-climbing fish and sea mammals. Carnivorous plants. Wingless birds and flying squirrels. What a glorious world this was."

"Can you help us?" the rorqual asked plaintively; the call of a whale can be most doleful.

"Can you swim through the skies?" Vith inquired with a smile.

"You know we cannot."

"Then you'll have to take your water with you. Do you know the man legend of Noah and his family? No, of course you don't. Another one of my ancestor's foolish meddlings. The principle is this: I can't save you all, but I'll take representatives of every species, in pairs, so the race will survive. This means that only a very few will live."

"No whale is immortal; we each have a time. But the song will not end. That is all we can ask. How is it to be done? I must report to others who await your word."

"There is a planet I'd like to tell you about. It is entirely covered with water. There are no land masses and no land creatures. All the creatures of the waters are peaceful vegetarians who live on a protein-rich algae that grows at the poles, breaks loose, and floats to the tropical waters in huge chunks. It's delightful, really. The main pleasures there are mating, singing, and acrobatics, both in and out of water. This planet revolves around a star in a galaxy many light-years from here, and for you, a long, long swim."

The rorqual was flustered. Vith spoke of concepts that her mind could not grasp. Vith saw her confusion.

"Relax, my sweet. You'll not have to leave your precious water, though your ancestors once walked the land. What made them turn back when everything else was clambering

to get out? Why did they return to the water when the earth
was a fruit ripe for the picking? Look at the results, I suppose.
For the whales, millions of years of peace. For men—"

"We have sympathy for the plight of men, even though
they have been so cruel to us. We ask only to live in peace."

"And so you shall. Lead me back to the others."

Once again Vith cruised out on a wave to greet the herds.
The surface was dotted from horizon to horizon with the puffy
spoutings of whales, as many others had remained with the
chosen few to see them off. There was no jostling for place
or contesting for right of passage, however. The decision was
made, and now all hopes rested with those selected for the
journey.

There were two enormous blue whales, two bowheads, a
half dozen sperm whales (a polygamous male and five fe-
males, a concession by Vith to practicality), two grays, two
narwhals, and so on. The lucky voyagers massed in the center
of the vast, encircling herds. At Vith's request a ring of open
water was established between the spectators and participants,
who began to swim, slowly at first, then with increasing
velocity, within the confines of the ring. The wind rose up
and the water began to rotate also, forming a maelstrom of
intense centrifugal force. The spinning funnel rose up into
the sky as a waterspout. Whales and water were all sucked
into the vortex and thrown into space. When the waterspout
cleared the Earth's atmosphere, it began to slow down, taking
the shape of a teardrop, the cetacean giants like tiny paramecia
in the droplet of seawater floating in space. Held together by
mutual suspension, the water molecules formed an elastic
surface tension that kept its shape intact. Whales swam through
the skies, as Vith had foretold.

Vith looked at what he had done, and he saw that it was
good. The whales were innocent victims; why should their
race die? They would feed and propagate and sing in their
floating bubble on a journey of many thousands of genera-

tions. They were now the size of lake trout, which was fitting because the small satellite that their water balloon would eventually splash into was scarcely a thousand miles in diameter. But for the diminutive cetaceans it was heaven indeed.

This mingling of two planetary waters occurred thousands of years in the future when Bertie, Vith, and everyone else had long since departed from Earth.

25

More Monkey

"The white-faced gibbon is known to sing in
the moonlight and at dawn."

—*Larousse Encyclopedia of Animals*

The Earth had been struck a terrible blow. She shuddered and
quaked from the savage shocks of the explosions. Her skin
scorched with radiation, her oceans' temperatures rising, her
atmosphere choked with deadly black ash, she was on the
verge of collapse. Her fabled regenerative powers depended
on balance. When all systems were out of balance at once,
there was no preventing disaster. But Mother Earth was very
large; she died slowly.

The detonations had been limited primarily to the four
continents of Europe, North America, Asia, and Australia,
although a number of wayward missiles landed randomly
around the globe. While Vith ministered to the whales Monkey decided to have a look around to see how other life was
faring in the aftermath of the destruction.

Since Vith was out wave-riding, Monkey borrowed his
cloud-seat and raced off to Africa to have a look at his cousins.

What he found there disturbed him greatly. Although very few bombs had landed anywhere near the grasses and jungles, prevailing winds had carried the radiation even to the far reaches of the Upper Nile, the Zambezi, and the Serengeti Plain. When Monkey touched down on the edge of a forest in Kenya, he noticed the dryness at once. Everything was covered with a film of dust.

He saw a band of black colobus monkeys. These creatures were once hunted almost out of existence for their long, silky coats. They normally spent many hours grooming each other, but now their fur was matted and dirty. They were listlessly picking at some rotten ground fruit instead of inhabiting the higher branches and feeding there, as they had done since time immemorial.

"My cousins!" cried Monkey, addressing the colobus in their own tongue. "What is the matter? Why do you not swing from the upper limbs, why are your coats not glossy and neat?" As Monkey approached, he saw that they were afflicted with a kind of mange from the radiation sickness, so that when they touched themselves, clumps of hair came away in their long, gnarly fingers.

On the plains the carcasses of millions of dead zebras and gazelles were putrifying, and this added to the spreading of disease, as cholera and plague germinated in the decomposing corpses. It attacked *life*, striking wherever it found a striving for existence. Plants, animals, birds, and reptiles all suffered equally. Only the insects, with their dense exoskeletons protecting their internal organs, endured and even thrived from the soundless poisoning.

"Cousins!" Monkey shouted, "it is I! *Monkey!* I can help you. Tell me what you need." As he spoke, Monkey saw that he could do nothing for the thousands and millions of suffering animals. Even Vith, the All-Knowing One, could save only a few score whales, and not many more humans. Monkey remembered that he owed his powers to Vith's ancestors.

"Come on now, pull yourselves together. Tell me, what regions, if any, have escaped the sickness?"

An elder came forward from the throng of colobus. He scratched at the place where he used to have a sagebeard. There was only a scabby sore.

"Are you a true monkey?" he asked.

"Yes, yes," screeched Monkey impatiently. "Where are the safe areas? I'll take you there."

"Men have it." The tribal elder's reply was simple and pointed.

"I should have known. Where are they?"

"Do not go there. It is a place of disease and death."

"The safe area! The safe area! Where is it?" Monkey ranted. He should have had more patience with the enfeebled, elderly colobus, whose monkey wits were scattered at the sight of his dying tribe. At last Monkey was able to coax from it the location of the nearest point where the radiation had not yet spread. The east face of a mountain in Kenya remained untainted, though on the west slopes vegetation had wilted, and nothing larger than beetles survived. On the east side of the mountain and only above an elevation of four thousand feet, a zone of relatively clean air and water remained. Unfortunately it was connected to the heavily populated lower areas by a road along which survivors had constantly fled, until the wooded areas and even the rocky patches above the treeline near the summit were overrun with people. This left no room for the animals who also were drawn to the place. A semblance of order was imposed on the spot by Kenyan government officials, who first roadblocked, and eventually dynamited, the road to the haven to prevent more émigrés.

When Monkey arrived, the makeshift camp was experiencing the problems of any concentration of refugees. There was not enough food and water. Sanitary conditions, never a strong point in Africa with its heat and its flies, were deteriorating. There was no medicine. There were two doctors for seventeen thousand people. The old forest monkey had been right. This was no place for them. Leaving the dismal scene at the mountainside camp, Monkey flew back to the forest below. He found the colobus in worse shape than when he left them. The heat of the day had taken its toll. The one with whom Monkey had conversed was now a stiffening corpse. Monkey stamped his feet in rage. His monkey brain didn't know whether to hate or pity the stupidity of men. He recalled the fancy speech he had given the night at Big Boys Camp. How prophetic he had been. The extent of the tragedy shocked even Monkey, who had been around long enough in various guises and incarnations to have seen plenty along those lines.

Even gods have their disappointments, thought Monkey. He was embarrassed to admit to the discouraged band that he could do nothing for them. Promising aid of some kind, he mounted his cloud-seat and rushed back across the steamy Atlantic to confront Vith.

"You too?" Vith sighed, looking tired after his exertions on behalf of the whales. "What do you expect me to do? Can I stand in front of the karmic wheel and tell it to stop? It would only run over me too. That foolish _____ _____, and you, and even Bertram Rupp, dear soul, you all want me to change the course of things. I am here merely as an observer—"

"But the whales!" Monkey interrupted.

"The whales had their own special destiny, especially their cousins the dolphins, of whom I sent several species. Fine, intelligent creatures they are, and none of the cruel streak in man."

"What about my cousins?" Monkey snarled. "Do you play favorites, then?"

"I am here as an observer," Vith repeated. "I observe that you have my seat, you rowdy animal. Give it back!"

"No!" shouted Monkey, who never liked being given orders.

"You restless, reckless ape, be careful or you'll get yourself thrown out of heaven again, like you did before."

"I don't care. It's not fair!" Monkey jumped up and down in his excitement.

"Very well, then I am going to attribute this outburst to your grief. I release you from your guardianship of Bertram for the time being. Do what you will here. Why don't you go see ＿＿＿＿ ＿＿＿＿? He's still trying to find a way; though I warn you, you'll only get yourself into more trouble."

"I might just do that," Monkey yelled, and he shot straight up into the sky.

Outside the van another arctic storm raged. Before the war, the precipitation would have been a fine, misty snow, piling up inch by inch until this area of Hudson Bay was covered to a depth of six or eight feet. Instead of a snowstorm, the downpour was a slushy rain mixed with hail, pitting the aluminum exteriors of the vans until they were pockmarked like big rectangular white golf balls. When the fiasco at the Bronx Zoo ended, and ＿＿＿＿ ＿＿＿＿ knew for certain that the war was near and that he was still going to be on the planet when it came, he fell back to his alternate plan, which was to drive north above the Arctic Circle to this remote hunting lodge, where ＿＿＿＿ ＿＿＿＿ used to hunt caribou, and hope that somehow he and the remnants of his force might survive the attack.

So far things had gone his way. The weather had been the worst part of the ordeal. For several weeks they had been completely isolated, the weather too severe for any movement or for radio reception. They stayed in the vans, or rather, ＿＿＿＿ ＿＿＿＿ stayed in his van and the others in the second vehicle, although they occasionally ate meals together.

If _____ _____ was miserable, it was not because of the loss of everything dear to him, all his personal and corporate possessions.

_____ _____ was hunched at the console of the onboard computer in his van, calculating the surviving assets of Accumulated Life for the seventh time. An accounts payable general ledger displayed on the screen; on the debit side was a monstrous figure representing, as near as _____ _____'s personal computer could calculate it, the amount, in dollars, of possible outstanding claims against the company, a figure in the hundreds of billions. He had no reason to believe that his private funds (Swiss francs and Krugerrands) existed anymore, so _____ _____ could only tally about four million dollars in convertible assets, represented mostly in the sophisticated electronics in the vans, and the contents of his money belt, which he never removed.

He was not worried, however. With a curious childlike glee, raising his hands off the keyboard and striking the letters with index fingers only, _____ _____ typed out the instruction:

RUN FORM 11111

The screen went blank for a moment, then the machine printed the message:

FORM SUCCESSFULLY STREAMED

_____ _____ typed in the command:

DISPLAY NEW BALANCE

Again the computer wiped its screen, paused, and replied:

ALL CLAIMS DENIED
LIABILITY = 0

Those innocent five digits in the upper right-hand corner of every Accumulated Life policy, never questioned, never challenged, were the basis for the company's final and absolute denial of each and every claim against it. Bertie Rupp accidentally got a copy along with a page of his treasured book. Only five other copies existed, or used to exist. To _____ _____'s knowledge, the version on his CD-Rom disk was the last remaining document.

_____ _____ was unhappy because he had no one to gloat with, no equal with whom to share his triumph of forms engineering. He was, then, ebullient and effusive when, returning from dinner one night in the other van, he found Monkey seated in his executive swivel chair.

"Monkey! What a surprise! How did you get in? No matter, I'm delighted to see you. I've just finished dinner. How about a brandy to warm us up?" _____ _____ moved cautiously around the computer carrel to the bar, remembering his last run-in with Monkey.

The animal in Monkey sensed the fear in _____ _____, and the amused ape bared his teeth with a laugh.

"Have no fear, Big Boy. I'm here to help you. Brandy would be nice."

"Where's your master?" _____ _____ asked.

"Vith is not my master!" Monkey screamed. "I'm free." He snatched at the proferred glass of brandy. Hurling it down in one gulp, he extended it crudely in a demand for more. He was obliged. "I've come on a mission of my own; I thought you might be of use to me, but now that I'm here, I doubt it. Is this all of you, these two cars?"

"Here, yes, but—" _____ _____ ad-libbed, looking for bargaining chips as he furiously tried to imagine what

Monkey could be up to. "I have no idea what's left in the world. Have you seen it? My company had substantial holdings all over the world—real estate, buildings, factories. What is it you want?"

"So many questions. To answer your first, I have seen only a portion of it. Little remains. This is a dying place, I have no more use for it."

"So then, you, too," probed _____ _____, "would like to leave?"

"There are other worlds to explore. Planets of great wealth and beauty. I have heard Vith—" Monkey stopped himself short when he saw the avaricious look on _____ _____'s face. Fallen angel though Monkey was, he was still a good monkey at heart. "Know this, Little Big Boy, it is I, Monkey, who gives the orders now. I decide. You will provide the materials. I will make us a machine, and if there is room for a few of you after I get all my cousins on board, perhaps I will be magnanimous."

"Of course, of course. Whatever you need. If only there was some way we could get hold of a copter or a plane, we could—hey, how did you get here, anyway?" _____ _____ wondered aloud. "We haven't been able to move for weeks."

"I have a little number outside that seats two," Monkey boasted.

"But my men?" _____ _____ asked. Monkey shrugged his shoulders.

"Leave them," he said. _____ _____ obeyed. The cloud-seat idled above them. Monkey and _____ _____ climbed up a ladder to the roof of the van, which doubled as observation platform and gun deck. From there they were able to hoist themselves onto the patiently hovering puff of vapor, and off they went.

_____ _____ could see no controls, nor could he make any sense of the unnatural solidity of the scud on which they sat. He sought to ask Monkey the thousand technical questions that presented themselves to his startled brain, but the ape was in a trance. His eyes crossed goofily in their sockets, and the expression on his face was inhuman, even for a monkey.

They soared up through dense, encircling, gray mists until they floated through the final layer of turbulence at thirty-five thousand feet. Monkey, shameless Monkey, who should have known better, was about to get himself kicked out of Paradise again. He would have done well to return to the aid of his charge, Bertie Rupp, who was about to enter the most difficult section of his ascent to Enlightenment, using no ropes, no pitons, no crampons: free-climbing.

26

Pluto's Helmet

Vith appeared in Bertie's camp after a week spent in quiescent bliss, recuperating from his labors. Transporting several cubic miles of seawater hundreds of light-years through space is not easy. As Bertie's guru, he felt obligated to show himself at regular intervals to allow Bertie a session of kensho, direct questioning of and by the pupil's teacher.

"You have done well, Bertram," Vith complimented his student, after Bertie had made obeisance before him. "I see that you have converted the camp to a school?"

"Of sorts; the kids couldn't play forever. They needed some structure. Tell me, are we all? I mean, are these children the whole future? It's so much responsibility. I feel like Noah."

Vith said nothing. He waited for Bertie's next question.

"What's it like out there? We all want to know. We can't stay here indefinitely. Can we?" Bertie asked. Vith gave him a brief description of the state of the world, including a summary both of his help to the whales and also of Monkey's shenanigans. All the while Vith could feel the unspoken question emanating from Bertie: Was there any way he could go take a look for himself?

"That irresponsible Monkey has my cloud device, but I suppose I could give you these winged shoes and this helmet," Vith mused, and Bertie jumped in surprise because he thought he'd kept his heart's desire a secret.

"Would you?" cried Bertie.

"This helmet gives its wearer the power of invisibility. Since you will be invisible, it will also protect you from the poison, as there will be nothing to irradiate. The benefits of the fleet feet should be obvious. However, I must warn you, there is a powerful side effect to the wearing of these sacred objects."

"What is that?" Bertie said, but he was trembling with anticipation, so he hardly listened when Vith responded.

"While these things will allow you to travel over your own devastated world, they will also place you in contact with another realm, one with a life and power all its own. You must be careful there, for things are not always what they seem. It is the world of my ancestors and your gods, a domain where women may be changed into islands or doves, where men become flowers, where a monster may have one huge eye in the middle of its forehead or may have one hundred eyes, only two of which are asleep at a time. It is the province of Furies and Fates. Do you think you can find your way?"

Bertie shook his head vigorously. He hadn't taken in too much of what Vith had said, because his mind was fixed on one goal: He was going to Kansas to see for himself if Emily was dead.

Vith brought out the headgear and footwear. The shoes were of simple sewn leather, the renowned helmet no more than a piece of stretched hide that fastened under the neck. What made them remarkable were the wings of beaten gold attached to both articles. Clearly ornamental, they were of no use whatsoever in motive power, but as soon as Bertie put them on, he felt extremely light-headed, and the first thing he knew, he was airborne, drifting helplessly upward.

"Excellent, excellent!" Vith called to him. "You've got a good head for this sort of thing, Bertram. You'll go far. Now get control of yourself."

Bertie flailed with his arms and kicked with his legs but continued to spin aloft without direction. Finally he took a few deep breaths and steadied himself; he began to hover in place, a sublime feeling known on Earth only to a few species of birds. Then he twisted himself toward Kansas and began to drift.

"You've got it!" Vith signified, and he waved good-bye, for Bertie was rapidly disappearing from sight—literally and figuratively. He was almost over the horizon, and his body was fading like frost before the morning sun. In another instant he was gone.

Bertie soon mastered the mental mechanics of flying; it was as easy as walking. Invisibility was more difficult to adjust to, because a blind spot the size and shape of one's own body is a considerable handicap.

Vith neglected to tell Bertie that his invisibility did not extend to the animal world, nor to the realm of myth, so Bertie was understandably surprised when a trio of white swans matched his speed and then turned into lovely young Greek girls, floating along in their white chitons, their dark hair flowing behind them, their long, beautiful noses like those on statues of Aphrodite. They spoke to him in unison, like a Greek chorus, or like the six-inch-tall Japanese twins in *Mothra*.

"We bring you greetings from the world below,
O son of man with heart of love and grace.
Ask any thing of us and it shall be."

"I wish the war had never happened," Bertie wished with all his might.

"Just Future wishes are possible.
So wish again, again, O favored one."

"I wish that only the evil die and the good survive."

The nymphs looked depressed. They huddled. They conferred. The center sprite broke formation to fly up closer to Bertie.

"Please don't make such impossible demands, Bertie Bertie. If the gods think you are mocking them, they'll make you perform difficult labors and you'll never get where you're going. Now, how about three nice, attainable wishes? Is there a monster you need slain? How about transformations? We can change you or anyone into just about anything."

"Can you bring a person, just one, back from the dead?" Bertie pleaded. The nymphs assumed identical downcast expressions. Then the one who had spoken brightened.

"No, Bertie Bertie, we can't, but we could take you to see Emily." By this time Bertie was wise enough not to question that the nymphs knew his name and the identity of his beloved. "Travel to the nether world is dangerous," the girl continued. "Are you sure you are willing to risk the journey?"

Bertie did not hesitate. "I am."

"Very well. Follow us Bertie Bertie, Seeker among the Dead." With that the three nymphs became swans again and flew toward the west, with Bertie in pursuit. They winged their way so swiftly that Bertie lost sight of them. He dropped down out of the clouds to get his bearings. By dead reckoning, Bertie figured he should be over Ohio, but the landscape beneath him didn't look like anyplace in the Midwest. In fact, it resembled the oddly motionless, lush carpet of the Brazilian jungle. Beneath him was a dark forest broken by a line of a river. The dense wood stretched as far as Bertie could see in any direction; the silver band of the water sliced through it from horizon to horizon. Bertie landed on the river's narrow bank. Again Bertie noticed the peculiar clarity and stillness of the water. It seemed not to flow in either direction, yet it was not stagnant. Bertie leaned down to take a sip from the stream, and giggled at the unexpected reflection of himself with wings on his head. He was wondering why he could see himself when a voice spoke to him and he jumped back in fright.

"I wouldn't do that if I were you." Bertie spun around. He was alone.

"Who is it?" he whispered timidly.

"Acheron here, son of Ceres, at your service."

"Where are you?" Bertie asked.

"I'm the river. And whom might I be addressing? What god are you?"

"No god. A man." Bertie gave his name.

"A mortal? None have come this way in many years. What brings you here?"

"I was following three swans who were to lead me—"

"Ah, yes," the river said, interrupting him, "they passed through only moments ago. Would you like me to call the ferryman for you?"

Bertie should have known who the river was talking about. When he was in the third grade, his very best elementary school teacher, Miss Mahaney, had made a wonderland of the classics, enchanting her pupils with the fantastic exploits of the gods among men, which of course, was why Vith had chosen this arena as the next testing ground in Bertie's battle for Liberation.

"Why are you a river?" Bertie asked, reasonably enough, he thought.

However, the body of water snapped back at him huffily. "I wasn't always a river, but I had the misfortune to back the Titans in their war against the gods. You would have, too, if you'd seen those giants. Well, they lost. The gods were too clever. So here I am. But I suppose I'm better off than my cousin Persephone. For eating a silly pomegranate seed she's condemned to spend half her time in the lower world. By the way, shall I get the ferryman? That is why you're here, isn't it? No one comes to see me unless they want to travel there."

"Is that the only way?" Bertie asked.

"The one and only way. Ah, here he comes now. He must have been expecting you." As the river spoke, a huge, black, three-headed dog appeared out of the foliage, all three jaws open and snarling, neck and shoulder muscles straining against the triple collar at the end of a chain leash held by Charon, the ferryman.

"My obolus, please." Charon extended a dirty palm open and upward. He was a filthy old man with matted beard and ragged cloak.

"What?" said Bertie.

"My obolus. My payment. One sixth of a drachma. You don't expect to ride for free, do you?" Charon demanded. Bertie was embarrassed. He was carrying no money, nor anything else of value except the helmet and shoes with which he dared not part. He searched his pockets, then remembered the small bag he wore around his neck.

"All I have is this," Bertie said.

"What is it?"

"A magic black-hole marble." Bertie offered it to the suspicious boatman, who took it and examined it. Then he began to laugh, and his laugh grew until it was a howl.

"Accepted," he shouted. "Get in, get in," he ordered Bertie, and for the first time Bertie noticed the peculiar bottomless boat that rested on the surface of the tranquil stream.

"Couldn't I just fly over?" Bertie asked.

"That would never do. Cerberus wouldn't like it." Charon gestured toward the hideous, menacing dog. "It is his job to guard the gates of Hell. Only those escorted by me are safe.

And though it is not right for me to carry the living in my boat, an exception has been made in your case. Besides, there is much you can learn, even from a simple boatman. In, Cerberus," he commanded, and the monster leapt onto a seat in the boat. Bertie followed reluctantly.

"My father is Erebus, son of Chaos. He is the dread darkness." Charon pushed off from the bank, poling the boat like a raft. Bertie saw that the water barely rippled as the stick dipped in and out of it, and he had the distinct sensation that they were not floating on the water but hovering inches above it. Strangely enough, as they proceeded toward the opposite shore, it receded away from them, until the tiny river had become a vast lake whose other shore Bertie could not see.

"Acheron, are you there?" Bertie called out to the first being he had encountered.

Charon replied. "This is now Acherusia, the lake that leads to Hell. I hope you have permission to be wearing that helmet and those sandals, for you are about to meet their owner, the ruler of the underworld, my boss, Pluto. This is his dog," Charon continued, patting the bristling hairs on the middle neck of the deformed beast, "and there, ahead, are his infernal regions."

A far shore had come into view. It was a black forest like the one they had left, except that the clouds hung low over it, and smoke from the open fires rose up and mingled with the vapor to form a hazy pall. Fires seemed to be burning everywhere up and down the shoreline, yet the smoke never drifted out over the water but curtained the interior from sight.

Pluto was in a rage in his chambers. He was displeased with Bertie on at least three counts. First, he objected to anyone wearing his precious possessions, but he had deferred to Vith's superior powers when the request had come in. Secondly, Bertie's incessant prayers and supplications had saved several people from his grasp. The Lord of the Dead was not a figure to be trifled with. Finally, Pluto had overheard

Bertie's futile wishes and mistaken them for mockery, as the nymphs had feared.

"Mortals!" he stormed. "They ignore us for hundreds of years, then the first one to arrive makes light of our powers with his ridiculous, impossible demands. I'll show him. I'll set him to some tasks that will test his mettle."

On and on he raved, cursing at his servants, throwing things, lashing out at the slimy denizens that crawled and slithered everywhere in his quarters and elsewhere in his kingdom. By the time Bertie was announced, he had worked himself up into a hellish fury.

Bertie had been escorted by Charon from the ferry into the forest and through the gloomy mists to the massive redoubt of the castle of the King of the Dead. Cerberus bounded ahead. The whole setting—the forest; the rock-walled, moated fortress; even Charon's manner of speaking—seemed more medieval than Greek or Roman to Bertie. He mentioned this to Charon as they crossed the drawbridge and entered the abode of the dead.

"There is some truth to what you say. The English were the last people to hear of us, read us, bring us to life and power again. Their imagination put a tinge on us. Today we are forgotten. That's why you have caused such excitement in coming here."

"I have?" said Bertie.

"Oh, yes. But I fear for you, my friend. Pluto may not want to let you go. As long as you are here, we retain our influence. But make no mistake, we are older than the British and their petty empire. We are the gods who first emerged from Chaos, the unfathomable abyss."

Bertie was surprised to find that a deity would have a sense of history and also knowledge of current events, but he understood Charon's warning.

"Welcome to Hell!" shouted Pluto from his throne when Bertie entered the royal hall for an audience with the King of the Dead. Cerberus lay at his feet, gnawing on a couple of human thighbones and a skull.

Bertie shivered when he saw this, and Pluto, noting his reaction, laughed from the depths of his heart-without-pity.

"My dog has an evil habit. He greets those who enter with friendly wags of the tail, but he attacks those who try to leave."

"He growled at me," Bertie responded.

"Really? Well perhaps today you are fated to escape my grasp, but not forever. And certainly not right away. We want to keep you here with us. Now, why are you here, other than to shame old Pluto by wearing his magic?"

"I came to see Emily Butterworth." Bertie decided a direct approach was the safest one in his present circumstances.

"She is not here. She is in another part of my domain, known as Kansas." Bertie's heart soared for an instant. "You mean, she's still in the world, alive? Oh, I should have kept going. I should never have followed those swans, or whatever they were—"

"Silence!" Pluto, Lord of Hades, cut off the tearful Bertie. "You did not hear me. I said she was an inhabitant of my realm now. Kansas is Hell. Remember the words of Marlowe: 'Where we are is hell, and where hell is, there must we ever be.' These words were never truer than they are today. *Wait!*" Pluto called out to the impetuous Bertie, who had turned to leave in disrespectful haste, as he had thoughts only of Kansas. "Do you think it will be so easy, puny mortal? Shall I send my legions against you? Disease, Fear, Hunger, and Poverty wait at the threshold for their chance at you. War, the bringer of Death, though sated from his recent gorging, could be induced to make a second appearance!"

"No, please!" begged Bertie.

"That is better. We would like you to stay here with us awhile. Why, you know only thirty or forty of the major deities. There are hundreds and hundreds of us, each with stories to tell. If you want to leave us, you'll have to win your freedom." Pluto sat back with a satisfied leer on his face. He had done his part in preparing Bertie for his greatest tests.

"How would I do that?" Bertie asked.

"The traditional way. Three labors. You should consider yourself lucky. Eurysteus gave Hercules twelve. For accomplishing them, Hercules gained immortality. However, if you can accomplish these small feats, I will let you see your Emily Butterworth—and more. I will grant you a page from the divine Book you seek."

"You have it?" Bertie gasped in astonishment.

"Don't act so surprised, boy. We have all texts relevant to our domain. Did I not just quote from *Faust*? We have an extensive library, from the Sybilline Books on down. But I doubt that you will ever see it—or your sweetheart, either— because I don't think you've got the backbone for the work."

"What must I do?" Bertie's voice was firm. He had grown much since the start of his journey.

Pluto rubbed his hands together, and he glowered at Bertie from his throne. It was obvious that he thoroughly enjoyed assigning the chores.

"Very well, then. First, I have heard it said that in a new part of my domain known as San Francisco, a miraculous tree grows. Bring me a seed from that tree and one of your tasks will be done. Do not go looking for your beloved. Remember the fates of Orpheus and Eurydice, and also those of Lot and Lot's wife. Do not disobey the gods."

In this way Pluto put Bertie to the test with a challenge and a temptation. Pluto signaled that the interview was over. Bertie was escorted by Charon up a long spiral staircase that led upward and broke through the ground like a rabbit hole, not far from the river's edge.

"Now you may fly to fulfill your first mission. Let me

caution you, as Pluto did," Charon warned. "Do not submit to your heart's impulse. Do things in their proper order and watch the timing."

Bertie ascended and to his surprise recognized the ground he was flying over as western Ohio. He soon located the fragmented vestiges of Route 80 and again followed it west, passing over the rubble of Toledo, Davenport, Des Moines. The helmet and shoes gave Bertie the speed of the gods, that exquisite compression of time and distance. In a short while he was clearing the Sierras and making his descent toward the Bay Area.

The first thing he noticed was the Golden Gate. Once again it was open to the sea, and instinctively Bertie liked it better. It was free of the bridge, which had been completely washed away by the ensuing tidal wave.

The Gate stood as it had for thousands of years before the arrival of men. Even the concrete bases at the feet of the towers were gone. The Twin Peaks tower lay crazily on its side like a fallen giant.

San Francisco had been ground zero. The Naval Weapons Station at Alameda, the Richmond Refineries, the Mint, the ships and submarines at port, all were targets. In addition, there was the Livermore Lab to the east, the high-technology belt in the Cupertino/Santa Clara area to the south, the research center at Stanford in Palo Alto, and many other sites that had been designated for destruction.

The city skyline had been destroyed by fire storms. The pyramid-shaped Transamerica building had completely vanished, although other structures remained as shattered shells.

It was difficult to get one's bearings in such an environment, but Bertie picked out the area near the Civic Center and landed there, among the ruins of City Hall and the Opera House.

There were no bodies in the street; they had been vaporized. Pluto was right, thought Bertie. This is his ghostly realm. Invisible and alone, Bertie walked up over the hill on Geary Street. At the top of this hill he could look out over the empty city. He turned to look down on Japantown to see if the Peace Pagoda had survived, but he saw instead an extraordinary sight: At the exact site of the Temple of Great Restraint a giant sequoia rose out of the ruins, standing tall and majestic. Bertie fell to his knees.

"This is the tree Pluto spoke of. I should have known." Bertie rose and went down the hill toward it. Singular in its vertical domination of the surrounding landscape, it was one of the largest trees Bertie had ever seen. It probably exceeded the legendary General Sherman in girth and height. Bertie walked around it, praying to it, and he was not at all surprised when it spoke to him in the voice of the Zen priest he had met so long ago.

"Yes. It's a miracle."

"Oh, no. Natural, very natural. Tell me, have you become One yet?"

Bertie didn't know how to reply. Certainly he was far down the road the priest had sent him on many months ago. He had survived the war. He had helped others. He had met another teacher in Vith Pankas. Several times he had seen glimpses or heard words from the Book. But he was not yet Liberated. There remained troubling, unanswered questions. And now he was bound to meet the requirements of an old god in his search for Emily.

"Your silence alone is an indication of great progress. You are not the timid, nervous person who forgot his sunglasses in his own coat pocket."

"I still don't have the Book."

"True, but you have already learned many of its secrets. Remember the Buddhist axiom: The purpose of all learning is to throw away the book."

"So many innocent people lost their lives. I can't justify

it. Emily—" Bertie was unable to continue, silenced by a wave of grief.

"Ah, the clinging of love. You are a changed person, aren't you? Listen well, adept. You have worked hard and traveled far to rid yourself of your evil misconceptions. Now you must work doubly hard to cast off your clinging to thoughts of love and compassion. Empty yourself of these notions and the Book will write itself in your mind's eye."

"I don't see how it's wrong—" Bertie began to protest. The priest stopped him.

"You don't. That is right. To borrow from the realm under whose sway you now fall, you must be like the god Oceanus, who flows back into himself. But now you must go. From far off I hear the council of the silent, calling your name."

Bertie shuddered, because he heard it, too, if hearing is the right sense to use in receiving the languid, sirenlike, insistent summoning that tugged him in the direction of Hell.

"I have been asked to bring back a seed from—" Again Bertie failed to complete a sentence because he didn't know whether to say "from this tree" or "from you."

"Of course, come up and pick one." Bertie rose off the ground and selected a healthy sequoia cone. It weighed a good five pounds, was easily two feet long, and was as big around as a pumpkin. Cradling it in both arms, Bertie thanked his benefactor and said his good-byes. Anxious to complete his duties, Bertie did not detour from his path but retraced his skysteps hurriedly.

Soon he stood before Pluto.

"Very well, I accept this magic seed. You!" the god cried, and the palace gardener came forward. "Plant this at once in the Garden of Earthly Delights." Pluto turned his attention back to Bertie. "You have completed one simple task. The next will be more arduous. Bring me the skin of a monster."

"I don't know of any monsters," Bertie answered truthfully.

"What? Dare you answer the gods so irreverently? Find a monster and bring me its hide, or speak no more of seeing your loved one."

Bertie was about to answer that as a Buddhist he could kill nothing, not even a monster, when the swans appeared in Pluto's chambers and swooped down to flutter near Bertie's ear.

> "Fear not, compassionate one.
> You shall find a dragon soon and then,
> Forget not your remaining wishes."

Immediately they turned and flew out again with a rush of beating wings. Pluto, before whose pitiless gaze nothing goes unseen, was witness to all this.

"I see that you have some allies in the Upper World. Fine. But remember this: Here *my* power is dominant. Yes." As he spoke, Pluto began to laugh, a merciless, mocking laugh. "My legions are swelling. Hell is filling up. The forces of the light are on the wane; darkness is in ascendancy. Go look at your world and see if you don't agree!" Pluto's black laughter filled the hall. With a wave of his hand Pluto dismissed Bertie, who scurried out and up the same staircase to the Upper World as fast as he could.

Rising into the air, Bertie craned his neck eagerly in search of the friendly nymphs, but they were nowhere to be seen. Hovering indecisively, Bertie had no idea where to look for monsters. To his knowledge there were none. Modern sightings of creatures like the Loch Ness monster or the yeti had proved to be wishful thinking. Some lonely creature might have survived the last six hundred years of exploration of the remote regions of the earth without being detected, but now there was the additional threat of the war and ensuing related disasters.

Absorbed in his thoughts, Bertie remained stationary like a human helicopter, oblivious to the approaching thunderhead that crept up behind him and gave him such a shove that he tumbled out of control, swept along by the force of the storm. Bertie frantically righted himself and tried to climb out of the black, rain-laden, highly charged cloud bank, but he was unable to free himself from its immense swirling power. When the tempest tossed him softly onto the sandy beach of an unknown shore, even Bertie knew that Zeus, the cloud-gatherer, the thunderer, had entered the game.

For a long time Bertie lay stunned where he fell. He had no idea how far he had traveled nor in which direction. To tell the truth, while Bertie wore the sacred helmet he had a less than precise notion of time and place; in myth they are less absolute, more elastic and changeable.

Bertie sat up. His scalp and skin were gritty with sand, but he was unharmed. The beach was tropical-looking but he could hardly smell the sea. Bertie was just about positive it was the Pacific Ocean because he had learned long ago that the Atlantic was much saltier, and so the air above it was more saline. Other than that bit of guessing, he was lost.

Because he was not a zoologist like Vith Pankas, Bertie didn't know that there was one true dragon left in the world, an authentic descendant of the dinosaurs, the giant monitor lizard *Varanus komodoensis*, known as the Komodo dragon. Bertie now lay on the shore of a small island in the Lesser Sundas, not Komodo itself but one of the nearby islands.

The Indonesian archipelago suffered little from direct nuclear attack but greatly from the aftermath of tidal waves, typhoons, and poisonous fallout on the wind. The dragons had been hunted nearly to extinction by poachers who prized their teeth as an aphrodisiac. Now they were further menaced by the extreme changes in temperature. Reptiles do not have the flexibility and adaptability of mammals to environmental change. On this island there were half a dozen dragons re-

maining, led by a venerable fellow over twelve feet long. At
this moment he was observing the seated figure of Bertie
from a rocky ledge above the water.

Two nights ago the dragon had had a prophetic dream in
which he foresaw his death. In the dream he had seen himself
in the air. With movements made slow by age, the giant lizard
edged off the rocks and onto the sand, his powerful tail
slithering behind him.

Bertie was absorbed in watching the crashing surf and
heard nothing until the broad tail lashed out and tumbled him
in a somersault onto his back. A moment later the dragon
had Bertie pinned to the sand with the length of his scaly
body, horny claws holding down each arm, its horrible head
hanging over Bertie's face, a cold eye fixed upon him, the
toothy jaw slightly open, the long, slender forked tongue
snapping out and back like a party favor.

By now Bertie was in the habit of conversing with gods
and animals. He called out to the dragon, but it seemed to
ignore him. Instead it raised its head and looked around, the
way many animals do when they have captured their prey.
Bertie squirmed and struggled, but the lizard had him restrained as securely as if he were back at Bellevue.

"I wish this dragon understood me," Bertie muttered to
himself, and at once the dragon responded.

"You're here to kill me."

"Oh, no," Bertie answered, realizing that he had just expended his second wish. He ought to be more careful and
selective with the precious last one, he thought to himself.
"I would never harm you," said Bertie, still flat on his back
under several hundred pounds of musty-smelling reptile.

"It was all in my dream. We dragons dream prolifically,
did you know that? Must have something to do with our diet.
I saw my corpse being carried away through the sky. Now
you have come, and I suspect from the air, since you wear
wings and you don't look like much of a swimmer. Is it my

teeth you covet? Do you want to make a pair of shoes or a wallet from my hide?"

Gentle Bertie was horrified at the idea and wanted to protest, but the dragon would have none of it.

"Here, look for yourself." It opened its elaborate, spring-loaded jaw to exhibit rows of fierce teeth. "I'm sure there isn't a sound tooth in my head, and my hide is scarred from years of fighting and mating and scraping along these rocks. You couldn't get one decent handbag off the whole piece. Why don't you go away and leave me to die in peace?"

"The god of the underworld sent me to get a monster's skin, but I wouldn't kill anything, and my nymph friends told me they would help me, but then they disappeared and I got caught in a storm—I think it was Zeus—and blown here to your island. You hunted me, I didn't hunt you." Bertie managed to get all that out while the lizard reared again to survey his surroundings.

"To tell the truth"—the lizard spoke to him confidentially, though he continued to sit on Bertie's chest—"I haven't been feeling too good lately. I think it was a wild pig I had a couple of weeks ago. Tough. Didn't go down right. Or maybe it was my cousin—"

"Cousin?" said Bertie in spite of himself. It was rude to interrupt, and Bertie felt it was important to be polite to the dragon, but he was curious.

"Yes, we dragons are cannibals. We eat each other. A gruesome, compulsive habit. I've always thought it's not the way I want to go." The dragon arched and looked around again, evincing the constant alertness that must be maintained in the dangerous natural world.

"We'd better get off the beach. You're sure you're not here to slay me?"

"Absolutely not."

"All right, then I'll let you up. But no funny business."

Bertie accompanied the petulant and friendly (for a dragon)

dragon to his lair, a smelly den in the rocks above the beach. In one corner was a pile of bones, some with pieces of dried flesh and hair still clinging to them. Bertie didn't have to be an anatomist to recognize human parts in the collection.

"Care for a snack?" the dragon asked solicitously.

"I'm a vegetarian," Bertie answered.

"No food for you here, then. Some of my relatives are leaf-eaters. I never could see it for myself. Nothing like a good pork loin for me. Now I must lie down. My digestive tract is really bothering me. You don't have anything for it, do you?"

"Gee, I wish I did," Bertie murmured, and at once a small goblet appeared in his hand, containing a ruby-colored liquid that sparkled and fizzed. Crestfallen that he had used up his three wishes in such a careless way, Bertie nevertheless took the magic potion and poured it into the sick dragon's mouth.

At once the reptile began to molt, and the skin sloughed off a beautiful white horse no larger than a Shetland pony. The dragon skin lay on the ground like a taxidermist's dream, while the newly emerged horse pranced around on the rocks, its shoeless hooves clattering gaily.

"How can I ever thank you?" the horse said to Bertie. "For thousands of years I've been trapped in that body and cursed that I could not even speak of what I'd once been. Now I can go back to heaven and be with my brothers and sisters, the gods. My punishment is over."

"Why were you being punished?" Bertie asked. The horse snorted.

"A small insolence to Pallas Athena, for which the lightning-thrower took offense and changed me into a dragon and cast me among these devils. It was a struggle just to survive, let me tell you. Here"— the creature kicked and pawed at its former hide—"take this skin back to Pluto. Tell him he can have the body but not the spirit." Without another word the horse galloped up into the sky and disappeared from sight, leaving Bertie by himself.

Bertie might have stayed on the island for a while to catch his breath from the tumultuous pace of his recent events, but at that moment two of the true dragons of the place poked their stony visages over the rim of the lair. Bertie snatched up the skin and took off, almost crashing from his unsteady state.

Crossing the Pacific with the speed of legend, Bertie returned to the hole beside the river that led to Hell. Soon he stood again before dark-haired Pluto.

"I've brought the dragon's skin," Bertie said, holding the parched, brittle shell in front of him with both hands.

"Yes, and you've meddled in the gods' handiwork again. Next you'll be helping Sisyphus push his rock or giving Ixion a drink of water." Pluto snorted. "Now we come to the third labor. All you have to do to satisfy me is answer the following question:

> 'Where is a man who falls but does not land,
> Who speaks but makes no sound,
> Who runs but does not move?'"

Pluto's words echoed in the ghostly emptiness of the throne room. Bertie trembled and tried to focus his wandering, exhausted consciousness on the meaning of the riddle. The helmet had become heavy on his head, and he longed to take it off but feared the consequences. So he tried to think about places where one could fall but not land. Outer space, maybe; yes, Bertie thought, you fall but don't land, and you run but don't go anywhere if you're floating weightless, but you can talk. Under water? You can't talk very well, but if you fall in, you generally sink and land on the bottom. He was so

tired, and it was so hard to think. All he wanted to do was
sleep.

Then Miss Mahaney's efforts of so many years ago paid
off for Bertie, because he suddenly remembered that the brother
of Death was Sleep, who sent Dreams to men.

"In a dream," Bertie said softly, almost to himself, and
Pluto asked him to repeat his words.

"In a dream you fall but never reach bottom; you try to
speak but you can't, or you forget what you're supposed to
say; and sometimes your legs get so heavy, you can't run,
no matter how hard you strain."

"True. Now, as I promised, you are entitled to your double
reward. First, I will present you with a single sheet from the
Book. Is there any section you are particularly interested in?"

Bertie didn't know what to say. He had only seen two
other pages from It and heard portions of one other page read
by Vith in New York.

"The future."

"I see. You'd like something along the lines of the Biblical
Book of Isaiah. Let's take a look." Pluto summoned an at-
tendant, gave instructions, and leaned back with a grimly
satisfied look on his face. The servant departed and returned
almost immediately with a thin leather pouch. Pluto motioned
Bertie forward.

"Take this but do not read it here. You must be gone now,
to Kansas, to see your Emily. Good-bye for now."

"For now?" Bertie asked aloud but absentmindedly, as his
heart was halfway to Kansas already, and his fingers played
at the clasp of the pouch.

"All mortals come to me in the end. No exception will be
made in your case. The whole earth is doomed to suffer the
fate of Atlantis, and for the same reasons. Now, off to Kansas
with you. You'll find it right where it used to be, only now
it is under my sway."

Pluto's laughter rumbled through the cave. Bertie shut his

eyes and stopped up his ears from the horrible sound, but the noise grew louder and louder until it shook the earth. The cavern suddenly collapsed all around Bertie, who fainted.

When he awoke, he found himself on the bank of the river where he had first entered Hell, but the rabbit hole was gone and the ferryman was nowhere to be seen. The jungle vegetation had been replaced with meadow grass. He called out to Acheron, but the stream was silent. The way things appeared and disappeared in this part of the world, Bertie decided he had better read his hard-earned page while he still had it, so instead of taking off, he sat down, took the pouch from around his neck, and opened it carefully.

This is what he read:

THE BOOK OF FUTURES

THE FUTURE IS A LONG FLY BALL, CURVING FOUL.

IT IS EASIER FOR A CAMEL TO PASS THROUGH THE EYE OF A NEEDLE THAN FOR A RICH MAN TO ENTER THE KINGDOM OF HEAVEN: NO PURCHASE NECESSARY.

BUY LOW, SELL HIGH: THE BEST THINGS IN LIFE ARE FREE.

THE DAY THE WORLD ENDED, PORK BELLY FUTURES WERE HOLDING SOLID AT 89.12.

MAITREYA, THE FUTURE BUDDHA, WHO KNOWS AND SEES ALL THINGS, IS DISPLEASED WITH MEN. SHE COMES

**NOT TO BRING PEACE BUT WITH A
SWORD.**

**CLOSEOUT! EVERYTHING MUST GO!
ALL SALES ARE FINAL.**

There wasn't much to the chapter, Bertie noted. Either it's
author hadn't been able to see very far into the future or else
the future was as brief and grim as was written. For a long
while Bertie sat and contemplated the esoteric and subtle
meaning of the bold words. Then he refolded the sheet of
paper and placed it back in its pouch.

Once more he ascended the clouds; once more he cast
around for his bearings and soon found Route 70, above
southwestern Ohio, which if he followed it would bring him
all the way to Kansas. Just as along Route 80 on his way to
San Francisco, Bertie found ruined city after city along his
route: Indianapolis, Terre Haute, Kansas City, Topeka, Salina.
Each one was now a huge crater, sometimes a half mile across,
extending in concentric rings of destruction, from completely
pulverized rubble to less complete devastation. From high
above Bertie could occasionally see a few tiny figures at the
extreme edges of the carnage, but the cities themselves appeared completely deserted. Bertie didn't know whether those
he saw were citizens of Pluto's empire or survivors.

When he reached Hays, Kansas, Bertie got off Route 70
and turned due south on Route 183, which would take him
all the way to Coldwater. It was fall. The corn should have
been high on its stalk, the wheat waving on the former prairie
for hundreds of miles in all directions, but instead there was
either blackened earth from fires or wilted crops rotting un-
tended in the fields. No birds picked at the heads because
there were no birds. Some hardy insects feasted. They were
the inheritors.

There was no sign of the farm, not even a remnant of a wall or a foundation. Bertie could only guess where he should land. Easing himself down to earth, Bertie stood once again in the grand silence of the plains, an area so vast that the early settlers abandoned their word *meadow* for the French *prairie*, which better suggested the immenseness of the range. In front of him the despoiled farmland was barren. The wind played over an unbroken expanse of nothingness.

Bertie was the only human in hundreds of miles. Due to the concentration of missile sites like the one from which Reggie Wilson had launched his attack on Carl Renstrom, this part of Kansas had been heavily bombed. It seemed foolish to call out for Emily in the wasteland, but Pluto had told him she was here, and Bertie hadn't yet quite rid himself of the very human notion that since she had died here, her soul must be lurking around somewhere nearby.

He lamented his frivolous expenditure of wishes. He wished he had another wish so that he might be able to conjure her up out of the exploded dust of the Butterworth farm.

As Bertie sat alone with his thoughts on the Kansas plain, the spirit of Emily came to him.

"Bertie, sweetheart, it is I."

"Where are you?" Bertie asked, but he did not look around because he knew better.

"Gone to the other side, safely gone over to the other side, thank heaven."

"Was it . . . bad?"

"I don't even remember," Emily replied honestly. "One minute I was writing you a letter and then there was a bright light, and since then I've wandered some. I heard you chanting my name, strange rituals I know nothing of. We knew each other so briefly, Bertie, dear."

"I know, Emily."

"You didn't mean it, I'm sure, but your prayers have kept

me from resting, longer than if you hadn't said them. Your grief, too, keeps me from my sleep."

"If only there was some way..." Bertie began, but he knew he had to accept her death. He had learned there were some things one could not change, and that his resistance was holding her back.

He could think of nothing to say to her. She knew he loved her, but they had no future. What were words in the face of that?

With bowed head Bertie sat by himself for one day, then a second, then a third. He thought of love, and bereaved lovers. He wished he had a remembrance of Emily. Around him the prairie wind kicked up funnels of dust that skidded like tops over the terrain. The sun rose and set, the moon rose and set, the stars appeared and disappeared—three times. Then Bertie thought of Adonis and said, "I wish Emily were a flower." His voice in the desert sounded weak and plaintive. He lay down and shut his glazed eyes and fell asleep. When he awoke, the field before him was carpeted with delicate yellow blossoms, their fragrance as rich as lilac or rose, tiny white pistils set in each flower like diamonds in gold settings. Bertie got up and walked among them, trying not to step on a single one. Their scent was overpowering in the air, like poppies. Though he couldn't bear to pick even one, Bertie picked up a few petals that had shaken loose in the breeze. He folded them in the page from the Book and put them in the leather pouch. Later he would dry and preserve them.

When Bertie returned to his remote sanctuary high in the Poconos, Vith was there to greet him. As soon as he landed, Bertie removed the helmet and stooped to unfasten the gold buckles of the winged sandals.

"Well done, Bertram. Are you then in such a hurry to leave Olympus?"

"I have a terrible headache," Bertie explained.

"Was the trip worthwhile, its resolution satisfactory?" Vith inquired.

"I'm still thinking about it," Bertie stated rather matter-of-factly, considering that he was addressing one whom he revered.

"You returned with some treasures, I understand. May I see them?"

Bertie withdrew the paper from which he carefully scooped the petals and put them into a clear plastic bag Vith handed him. Then he fully unfolded the paper. To his utter amazement it was blank.

"I don't understand. I can remember it all, so what's the point?"

"Perhaps the point is you don't deserve to have it if you can't remember it. But the greater lesson is that nothing returns from the other world."

"But the flowers—" Bertie protested.

"The flowers are a miracle from this world. May I hold that bag?" Vith sniffed its contents. "Very interesting. This would make a nice tea. Might even have medicinal properties. You ought to investigate that, Bertram."

"I will," Bertie replied, although at first he was horrified at the idea of boiling his treasure. "How is everyone here?" he asked.

"Restless. But you must have patience, Bertram. The time is not yet right. Besides, that troublesome Monkey is going to require my full attention in the near future."

After a few days he looked back on his excursion to the nether world almost as if he were recalling a dream. To keep the memory fresh, he wore around his neck, in the tiny silk pouch where he used to keep a shiny black marble, a few petals from the first post-holocaust plant, which Bertie named Emily.

27

Iron Monkey Jumps Into the Wisdom Fire Again

When Monkey ran amok in Chinese heaven six thousand years ago, one of his pranks was taking a bath in Lao Tzu's alchemical cauldron, where the venerable sage brewed the wine of the Immortals. This gave his skin its legendary hardness and, along with the nectar he drank of the life-giving elixir, made him immortal.

The superintelligence imparted to him so many millennia ago by Vith's ancestor was not transmitted to any descendants, because almost as soon as he received his altered brain, Monkey became an enlightened Buddhist and took a vow of celibacy.

His enhanced mind enabled him to understand effortlessly the complicated toys of man, their weapons and vehicles, their electronics and their mechanics. Such artificial devices were a source of amusement to one who, like Vith, moved freely through space. He tried to explain this to _____ _____ as they floated along.

"You mean," _____ _____ asked incredulously, "there's no engine or anything inside this cloud?"

"Absolutely not."

"Then why bring it, why have it at all?"

"One has to have someplace to sit down."

"But you can't..." and _____ _____ was going to say you can't sit on a cloud, but clearly they were sitting on one, as they jetted along above the eerily solid cloud-scape below. Instead, he asked, "Why sit?"

"To concentrate, fool! Oh, if only you had listened to me when I told you and your powerful friends how it would be if you didn't change your ways. Instead, you kept me in a cage. Now look at you, you hairless white ape, trembling and shivering before me! You monkey!" If Vith had been there, he would have strongly reproved Monkey for his dangerous tendency toward egotistic self-aggrandizement, the same mischievous trait that made him think he could best the forces of the Jade Emperor, and even Buddha himself, and be Master of Heaven, Great Monkey Sage.

"Where are we going?" _____ _____ wanted to know.

"Back to Africa, Big Boy. I've some unfinished business there."

"Hey! I've got some shares in a diamond consortium there. We need diamonds and rubies for lasers. Oh, and we should pick up some titanium while we're there. It's the only place you can get it."

"All in due time, little Big Boy. First I must tend to my tribe."

They flew along, each scheming to rid himself of the other when the moment came. Monkey hurried to his colobus, but it was too late for them. They were dead. The stench of carcasses was more than _____ _____ could take.

"Please, climb out of here, for God's sake! I can't bear it!"

Monkey's face was wild with rage, but he, too, was nauseated by the smell of death. He drifted upward until they were above the reach of the foul wind.

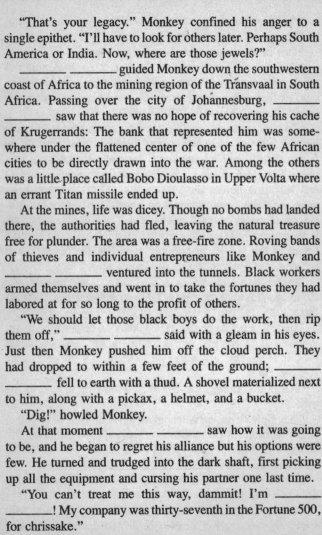

"That's your legacy." Monkey confined his anger to a single epithet. "I'll have to look for others later. Perhaps South America or India. Now, where are those jewels?"

_____ _____ guided Monkey down the southwestern coast of Africa to the mining region of the Transvaal in South Africa. Passing over the city of Johannesburg, _____ _____ saw that there was no hope of recovering his cache of Krugerrands: The bank that represented him was somewhere under the flattened center of one of the few African cities to be directly drawn into the war. Among the others was a little place called Bobo Dioulasso in Upper Volta where an errant Titan missile ended up.

At the mines, life was dicey. Though no bombs had landed there, the authorities had fled, leaving the natural treasure free for plunder. The area was a free-fire zone. Roving bands of thieves and individual entrepreneurs like Monkey and _____ _____ ventured into the tunnels. Black workers armed themselves and went in to take the fortunes they had labored at for so long to the profit of others.

"We should let those black boys do the work, then rip them off," _____ _____ said with a gleam in his eyes. Just then Monkey pushed him off the cloud perch. They had dropped to within a few feet of the ground; _____ _____ fell to earth with a thud. A shovel materialized next to him, along with a pickax, a helmet, and a bucket.

"Dig!" howled Monkey.

At that moment _____ _____ saw how it was going to be, and he began to regret his alliance but his options were few. He turned and trudged into the dark shaft, first picking up all the equipment and cursing his partner one last time.

"You can't treat me this way, dammit! I'm _____ _____! My company was thirty-seventh in the Fortune 500, for chrissake."

"I'm going to rehabilitate you and turn you into a good

communist, little Boy. Your first assignment is to dig! Now dig!"

In the diamond mines of South Africa, then in the bauxite mines of Jamaica, and again at some remote diggings in the southeast Australian desert, _____ _____ learned first-hand the working conditions required to fuel his high-technology existence. For the sleek aluminum skins on his private corporate jets men worked at absurdly low wages in the closeness and darkness of underground chambers. When they left the mines at the end of a shift, they looked like earth-men, men made of dirt and stone. As he hacked away at a wall of rock, _____ _____ remembered when he blamed the loss of a golf match on his irritation over having to grant the Jamaican bauxite miners a raise to sixty-five cents an hour.

Monkey was in his element. He had _____ _____ to do all his dirty work, he had Vith's skycart to race around in, and he was free. Yet he was troubled. Everywhere he went, the wildlife was dying off. It was beginning to look like men had caused the whole global ecostructure to disintegrate. The life-giving wind now spread poison. The oceans were in turmoil. The land lay barren. Monkey feared it was going to be like the time Vith had told him about, sixty million years ago, when some other aliens sprayed Earth with a massive dose of ethyl chloride to test a new planet-refrigeration system for cold storage and killed all the dinosaurs.

Monkey found a remnant band of Red Uakaris in the Amazon jungle, where prevailing winds had thus far spared them from the sickness. With the wisdom of animals they knew that something drastic had occurred, and they had retreated deeper into the nearly inaccessible reaches of the rain forest. Gregarious creatures, they exhibited an unusual moroseness when Monkey swooped down to save them. He called them together in the highest branches of a wide-trunked mangrove tree, not far from the mighty Amazon, greatest of all rivers on Earth.

"Brethren!" Monkey called out when the excitable group quieted down. "There has been a terrible calamity. Preparations are being made for an evacuation. Please assemble all your relatives for the trip."

"Leave the river?" the monkeys chattered to each other. "Leave our mother and father and protector and friend? Never!" They had not seen the effects of the holocaust to the north and could not imagine any calamity that would make it necessary for them to move.

"The river will die soon, and you with it, if you don't come with me."

"The river die? Impossible! The river is the source of all; look how the trees sink their roots in it. Land and river mingle together here. We will stay. The divine water will provide for us."

Monkey changed his tactics. "The river is All. You are right. But let me ask you this—is the river today the same as it was two full moons ago?" The monkeys coughed and sputtered nervously. This strange intruder who looked like some kind of monkey but flew in the sky like a bird, who knew their language but seemed also to know the ways of Man, had touched on the fear that had risen in the hearts of all the wildlife in this part of the Brazilian jungle: Something was wrong with the river. Twice in the past eight weeks the water had become undrinkable, as thousands of corpses floated from upriver, to the west.

"Man. It's Man again, isn't it?" Brazil was the site of one of the human race's most destructive environmental blunders. Spurred on by rabid American industrialists who saw a new wilderness for the taking in the late 1960s, the Brazilian government built a thirty-five-hundred-mile highway into the jungle and at the end of the road erected a modern city of skyscrapers, limited-access highways, hotels, and fast-food restaurants. This piece of inspired idiocy tore the jungle in two pieces, proved fatal to several Indian tribes, and brought thousands of treasure seekers into the backcountry in search of gold, copper, rubber, lumber, and other natural resources.

"Yes, Man. This time he has exceeded even his own worst imaginings. The Earth is dying. I have decided to colonize another planet"—for the first time Monkey spoke of his plan—"where monkeys will be the masters and all animals will follow them."

"We don't wish to rule the others. We only want to live in peace."

"Wise animals. I will be your lord and king, beneficent sage and gentle ruler. But you must come with me now, for time is short."

Far beneath them on the jungle floor, where the land was so saturated by the nearby river that it more closely resembled a swamp, the first signs of the disaster were becoming evident. A general migration had begun away from the contaminated areas to the north and west. Species usually not seen in the rain forest were appearing, and thus the carefully preserved balance of predators and prey was upset.

The Uakaris capitulated after some protracted squabbling. They accepted Monkey as their king and agreed to abide by his commands.

"I may call upon you to do some work for me," Monkey proclaimed.

"Work?" the innocent creatures asked.

"Yes, some light assembly, electronics, that kind of thing. Don't worry, it's easy. A chimpanzee could do it. I'll take care of all the heavy construction. Now just wait here while I go fetch my slave."

In short order Monkey set up a rocket factory, although it looked more like Santa's workshop than Lockheed as the monkeys dashed about, leaping on the worktables, hurling tools at each other, and scrambling for the fruits and dainties

Monkey fed them to keep them interested in their work. He
and _____ _____ made periodic foraging expeditions
for the raw materials required. Monkey had an innate understanding of the laws of physics, and this enabled him to take
many shortcuts in turning unfinished metal into gleaming
sheets, or transforming gooey muck from the deep underground into volatile missile fuel. _____ _____ knew
that if he could gain control of the mad ape, he could learn
most of the secrets of the universe from him.

As it was, however, Monkey ruled the roost. For the first
week of their stay in the humid jungle, _____ _____
suffered from diarrhea and vomiting, and he feared that somewhere he might have been exposed to the deadly radiation,
but it turned out to be common dysentery. He was on his
back for several days, while Monkey flew here and there for
necessary items. When _____ _____ gained enough
strength to enter the corrugated tin shed Monkey had hastily
erected, he was astounded at the progress that had been made.
Monkey's conception of the perfect missile was not funda-
mentally different from the fanciful creations of early science-
fiction filmmakers.

In other words, Monkey's rocket looked vaguely like a
1959 Cadillac stood on end, heavy on the fins and chrome,
constructed on a scale unimagined even in Detroit. The vehicle was being assembled horizontally, which only increased
the illusion that one was looking at an enormous wheelless
auto.

"Will it fly?" _____ _____ wondered.

"Oh, yes, wherever I want it to," said Monkey.

"And where is that?" _____ _____ asked slyly, but
Monkey wouldn't divulge his destination.

"When can I start to get my people together?"

"Your people?" Monkey mimicked _____ _____ with
brutal accuracy.

"Yes, I've made a few promises and I owe favors. I

was hoping to be able to take thirty or forty—" _____
_____ pleaded, but Monkey cut him off.

"You and your mate may go. That is all."

"But, but—that's not fair. You're taking hundreds of monkeys—"

"Correct!"

"I have no wife, mate," the dejected _____ _____
confessed. The exigencies of being a robber baron had left
him with little time for the entanglements of marriage. The
women he had known, mostly scheming secretaries with visions of power and wealth in their eyes, were all blown up,
along with the cities.

"You'd better find one before we go, or you'll have to
take a monkey for a wife," said Monkey, and he grinned
lecherously.

"Where?" _____ _____ asked despondently.

"There's always that Californian woman in the camp. We
could snatch her up. I'm sure she'd love to go to outer space
with you."

"The woman I saw with Rupp and the others at the zoo?
Damn, Monkey, you're right. Her husband is an idiot. I'd be
doing her a favor. Let's get her." In this way and with other
remorseless expressions, _____ _____ puffed himself
up to convince himself that he was justified in an act of
kidnapping.

Del and Bryce were already thinking along interplanetary
lines. The night before _____ _____ and Monkey plotted to kidnap her, Bryce had approached Vith about having
a baby by him. She thought of herself as a space-age Madonna.
Del was all for it. Vith demurred.

"The massive amounts of psychedelic chemicals you ingested have already transformed your fetus—yes, you are
pregnant, about eight weeks now, I'd say," Vith informed
her.

"It must have been the night we first saw you," Bryce said excitedly.

"Merely hearing my teachings has provided you with enough good energy to have a super baby," Vith said, trying to conform his words to the language of the Californian.

"I've got to go tell Del! Will he be surprised!" Bryce squealed. She hugged Vith and ran trippingly to her lover. Vith raised his head toward the sky in a gesture that conveyed his feelings across cosmic gaps of evolution and anatomy.

The next day Monkey swooped down like a bird and plucked Bryce out of camp as neatly as any falcon ever struck and soared. Bertie was still feeling the effects of Pluto's helmet when he witnessed the abduction. Thoughts of Leda and the god-swan muddled his perception as he watched the golden-haired woman go screaming and kicking into the sky. Then he caught sight of two familiar figures clasping the writhing woman to them as they darted off.

"Monkey!" he cried, "what are you doing? Come back!" His shouts were carried by the winds; they sent pangs of conscience through the fallen ape, but he didn't turn back, because he was still driven by accumulations of anger and resentment toward Vith.

Closing his ears to Bertie's pleadings, Monkey flew off with his captive. The cloud-seat was crowded with three aboard, especially when one of the three was an uncooperative passenger. Monkey had to concentrate very hard to develop enough thrust to carry them over the peaks of the Poconos. Finally he was forced to subdue the struggling Bryce with a sleep-inducing mudra. They veered south toward their temporary base in the Amazon jungle.

"Thornton Boyd, where are you now?" _____ _____ gloated into the teeth of the wind. Boyd had lost a billion dollars in Brazil, but not before he'd gashed and scarred the forest in search of a fortune in paper. He and _____ _____ were of a kind. They belonged to the same clubs.

In fact, the devouring capitalist was just finishing his Veal Oscar at his athletic club when Manhattan became incendiary.

Poor Monkey! His willfulness was leading him far astray. His simian tendencies toward curiosity and mischievousness were rising up and overwhelming his better, if alien, nature. At heart he knew that he was wrong, but he couldn't stop himself. His dislike for _____ _____ had fermented into a bitter hatred, but Monkey was bound to him by an alliance of necessity. He could see that it would be cruel to take _____ _____ alone and convinced himself that Bryce really wanted to go.

Monkey flew south over the ocean to avoid seeing the destruction, then west to pass over the shattered remains of Cape Canaveral. He had hoped to scavenge the place for components, but there was nothing left.

"Look there, Big Boy!" Monkey grimaced as he shouted, pointing at a gantry that stood stripped to its skeletal frame of I beams, like a lone monument. "Only a few decades ago one of my kind became the first primate in space. Bingo was his name. You sent us before you dared go yourselves."

When Bryce awoke, she found herself in a room full of monkeys. The only other human besides herself in the room was that awful _____ _____. She remembered being seized and being taken on a wild ride, and she remembered Monkey making a strange gesture in front of her, then she knew nothing until she opened her eyes and saw hundreds of monkeys running in circles and crawling all over a gigantic machine.

"Del!" she cried. The monkeys ignored her, but _____ _____ turned around.

"Welcome to Brazil. The last time I saw you was at the zoo, I think."

Bryce shook her head to clear the dregs of sleep. Her blond curls tossed back and forth. "I remember. Vith said you were—where's my husband? I want Del!" She started

to cry. Just then Monkey struggled in under a sack of microchips he's stripped from a Minuteman 2 that had sunk off the
Florida Keys. Flinging down the canvas bag, Monkey yelled,
"This is it. Everything we need to complete the rocket! Hey,
you Uakaris! Get to work. I've found some of your cousins,
langurs, who'll join up with us shortly!"

"More monkeys!" _____ _____ groaned.

"Ah, my human pets, how are you?" Monkey scarcely
glanced at them as he busily began to sort out the various
random memory chips, digital sensors, miniature amplifiers,
transformers, and microprocessors.

"I want to go back!" Bryce wailed. Monkey decided it
was time for him to have a talk with the woman.

"My dear," he began, trying to sound soothing and profound like Vith. "Sometimes life takes us strange places and
turns in unexpected directions. You have become necessary
to our venture into outer space and beyond. Are you willing to leave all earthly ties behind and join us? _____
_____ has selected you to be his mate, as we colonize—"

"But I'm pregnant already," Bryce gasped.

"Oh, dear," said Monkey. "This puts a different light on
things altogether. Now what do I do?" He was truly perplexed,
for the animal side of his nature reacted strongly to the
news.

"She goes, anyway," said _____ _____, who felt the
stirrings of desire as he watched Bryce wave her golden hair.
"It's too late to do anything about it now."

I'm not so sure, Monkey thought to himself, but aloud he
only said, "All right, let's get back to work. Young woman,
you come with me. I'm going to make you some herb tea."
Monkey took Bryce aside to have a few confidential words
with her.

The langurs were a beautiful race of monkey, with silver
hair and black markings. They are of the species *Hanuman*
and were sacred to the Hindu. Monkey himself was a *Han-*

uman. He'd returned to the mountainous regions of Nepal, and at altitudes above six thousand feet he'd found a few dismal survivors of the war. In their natural habitat in the high Nepalese forest the monkeys would have been relatively unaffected had not the wind patterns swept a devastating rain of fallout from the Soviet Union to the north onto their pristine jungle. Unprepared for such an onslaught, the langurs, as well as the wolves, tigers, elephants, and a myriad of other species, all succumbed.

The high-altitude teak forest had the same wilted, diseased look as other contaminated areas Monkey had seen. Everything was dead or dying. The chain of photosynthesis was disrupted. That process by which all life on earth was sustained, that thread on which the jewels of this tiny corner of Indra's net were strung, was asphyxiating Mother Earth.

Monkey took only healthy langurs, because the law of the jungle is that only the strong survive. In a thousand square miles of dense hardwood forest he could find only two dozen monkeys fit enough to travel. These he transported back to South America. The Old World and New World monkeys were fascinated by each other's appearances and habits. Thorough inspection by grooming followed, as well as the incessant chatter of monkey talk.

"Terrible, terrible, terrible! The evil wind came, our beautiful nuts and berries withered, the water turned bad"—here the Uakaris looked at each other knowingly—"then Death came. First the plants died, then the plant-eaters, then those who eat the plant-eaters."

"What did you do?" the Uakaris asked, their short, bushy tails twitching nervously.

"We climbed higher into the mountains, but Death followed us. When we were rescued by our great warrior king"—the langurs revered Monkey as an Immortal of their own kind—"we were at the upper reaches of the forest. Any higher and the trees give out. You, too, live in the treetops. You know what we say."

"Yes, how are we to live in that confining thing?" a Uakari howled, pointing to the nearly fully assembled rocket.

"Monkey says in space there's no up or down. When you jump, you don't stop or fall down, you just keep going. He says it will be fun."

"Our hard work is almost complete."

"We must go with Him or die."

"Yes!"

"It is so," different monkeys exclaimed, and a consensus was reached.

"At least in there we'll have no enemies," one pointed out. He was rebutted.

"What about that _____ _____? He looks like he would eat monkeys."

"He wouldn't stand a chance against all of us. Besides, our leader has him on a leash." This brought a storm of titters and chuckles from the excited creatures, who had never before seen a human submit to the will of an animal.

"Shhhh. Here he comes now!" they whispered to one another as _____ _____, Monkey, and Bryce came into the assembly area and climbed the short ladder into the ship. "He's not as fierce-looking as a leopard!" a langur proclaimed. The Uakaris involuntarily screeched their warning call. Monkeys have an intense fear of the big cats; when the langurs said *leopard*, the Uakaris saw jaguars.

When _____ _____ entered the spaceship for the first time, he discovered that the living cabins were constructed to monkey scale, about two-fifths human scale. By careful maneuvering he could squeeze down the low, narrow hallways, but he couldn't even enter the individual sleeping quarters.

"Dammit, Monkey! How am I—how are *we*—supposed to live in there?"

"Oh, I guess the little fellows got carried away. We'll knock out a wall or two for some living quarters, but the hallways you'll have to live with. All the wiring and structural supports run down the length of the ship to either side of those corridors, and I won't move them."

_____ _____ again caught a glimpse of how it was to be for him in the future, when he was locked inside the cramped shaceship for a long voyage with hundreds of unhousebroken monkeys. Having a beautiful woman on board would certainly ease the pain. Deep down in his jealous, paranoid mind, _____ _____ suspected that the design of the ship was deliberate. After all, the monkeys were working from that damn ape's blueprints. If he was to father a new race on a pioneer planet, he would have to endure hardship, as his forefathers had, _____ _____ thought to himself. He cast himself as a brave pilgrim carving settlements out of some exotic new world, and indeed, the mental analogy was not too far from the truth. If _____ _____ was let out in a fertile new territory, he would undoubtedly repeat the mistakes of his ancestors. Monkey had no intention of letting that happen. While he and _____ _____ stood arguing in the hatchway, Bryce found the newly installed ladies' room inside the rocket and locked herself in, saying that she wouldn't come out until she was promised she could see her husband.

While _____ _____ banged on the door and begged his new bride to come out, Monkey supervised the loading of provisions. Many tons of nuts, berries, and fruit were carted into the ship. _____ _____ took note of this as he paused in his flailings and pleadings.

"Isn't there any meat among the supplies?" he asked.

"Absolutely not. This is a Buddhist ship; these monkeys are good vegetarians—"

"So am I" came a muffled voice from the other side of the door.

"Come on out of there, for chrissake!" _____ _____ hollered, then he turned again to Monkey. "Give me a gun or something so I can go shoot a few steaks. I can't live on animal food, dammit."

Monkey frowned. "You'll get used to it. It's good for you."

"How long is this trip going to take? If you won't tell me where we're going, at least let me know that." Momentarily forgetting Bryce, _____ _____ plied Monkey with questions. "This baby looks pretty fast. What can she do?"

"We'll start at sixty-five!" Monkey answered.

"Oh, boy, that's sixty-five what?"

"Miles an hour."

"What! But . . . but at that rate it would take centuries, millennia to get anywhere!"

"So what? I'm immortal. I'm not in a hurry."

"What about these monkeys?"

"Their descendants will arrive. In the meantime there will be opportunity for instruction and improvement. After a few generations—"

"This is insane," _____ _____ shrieked. "I can't go with you! I'd be dead long before we ever— You bastard! You planned this! I'm leaving!"

It was an empty threat and both parties knew it. Where was he to go in the dense rain forest of the Amazon basin, where the only shelter was this primitive work shed? Under the glare of klieg lights installed for night work, _____ _____ realized that Monkey intended to make his life as miserable as possible. Unless the unwilling female on the other side of the door changed her mind, he would be doomed to spend the rest of his life without the benefit of human companionship. He renewed his effort at the door.

The monkeys, meanwhile, were on-loading the last of the provisions, while others took down the scaffolding around the vehicle. _____ _____ had always assumed that at some point it would have to be hoisted to vertical for liftoff, but he saw no crane or other device for accomplishing that maneuver. Furthermore, inside the ship there was no cockpit or control room; in fact, no evidence of controls of any kind, although Monkey had shown him a remote-control unit about the size of a pocket calculator. Monkey had told him that it was the operating panel for the whole machine, but _____ _____ hadn't believed him.

Once everyone was aboard, Monkey activated the hand-held toy that motivated the three-hundred-foot-long space-ship. It took off like a Hovercraft, rising straight up from the position on which it sat on Earth, but not in a cloud of dust and fuel vapor like an ordinary rocket. It seemed that Monkey only needed a few gallons to make the craft airborne, issued in delicate spurts of tiny engines mounted on the underbody. Once he achieved an altitude of twelve thousand feet, Monkey leveled off and cruised northward, because he had one more mission to accomplish on Earth.

The spacecraft itself was a flying marvel. It was capable of fantastically greater speeds than the humble sixty-five miles an hour Monkey had suggested, but for now Monkey was taking it on a test drive, not straining any system, shaking out the bugs for what would be a long space voyage, even at near the speed of light.

Back up the Atlantic coast they went, retracing their route of the previous day's kidnapping. More than two months had passed since the war, but little had changed since that awful day. No signs of reconstruction were in evidence. Shattered buildings lay where they fell; areas blackened by fire contin-ued to smolder; flooded cities stood awash in a stagnant backwater of ashes, soot, and debris.

Hardly a sign of life was visible. The eastern seaboard was once described as a megalopolis, a single great city from north of Boston to south of Washington, D.C., along both sides of Route 95 and the old Route 1. The band of total destruction more than covered it.

Monkey put the ship into a tight circling pattern over the Poconos. _____ _____, who was an avid sailor, had been plotting their position and progress. He recognized the ancient, worn-down mountain range from the air, and he began to suspect treachery. They were airborne and had the woman with them, and _____ _____ wanted to keep the status quo, as he had strove mightily to do all his life. He approached Monkey.

"Why are we back here? Why don't we go into orbit?" he demanded to know.

"All in good time," said Monkey. "Are you ready yet, my dear?" the ape called out to Bryce.

"Yes, I am" came the answer.

"All right, everybody stand back." Monkey cleared a path from the ladies' room to the main hatch. Bryce opened the door and emerged running. Monkey opened the hatchway door, and out she jumped, wearing a silver jumpsuit and a small parachute pack. _____ _____ was so surprised, he failed even to make the most futile of grabs for her. When he realized what had happened, he would have leapt to his death, but Monkey slammed the door in his face.

Bryce floated peacefully downward toward the camp, where she could see tiny figures running around in excitement and pointing upward. As she guided herself down, she felt a stirring in her belly, although it was too early for the baby to be moving. Her baby's first jump, she thought, and then she wondered if there might be some way to give birth in midair, on a jump. She'd have to talk to Del about that. And she'd be sure to put in a good word for Monkey with Vith. As much as she liked Monkey, she was glad to be away from the spaceship and its passenger list of monkeys and that horrid _____ _____.

At 13,500 feet Monkey circled steadily over the Poconos. His purpose fulfilled, he could now commence his epic journey through space, yet he lingered. He hungered for one last conversation with Vith. _____ _____ meanwhile suffered the tortures of the damned: From a sealed window he stared longingly at the green and grey textures of the Pennsylvania mountains.

28

Genesis, Exodus, Revelation

And it came to pass that the Earth expired. Her atmosphere burned away, her waters boiled up and evaporated. The tumultuous oceans, which ancient peoples thought to be infinite, proved their changeability like all other things. They became deserts. When the thin buffer of the upper stratosphere was removed by insidious radiation, life on Earth was doomed. This was the final blow from which the beautiful blue goddess could not recover.

The process would take several thousand years, but long before the last insect laid its arid exoskeleton out to dry, human history was ended. Earth became like Mars, a dead planet, barren and unprotected against the unremitting blast of the cosmic furnace.

Bertie had said how much he felt like Noah. The analogy was not lost on Vith, who at the time had said nothing. Once before, his ancestors had tried to cover their mistakes with an outpouring, a flood. The story is known in many versions, from Gilgamesh to Genesis to the story of Deucalion and Pyrrha. But the survivors of the flood had made an even bigger mess of things than their forebears. Now it was up to Vith to decide if the human race should continue to exist or whether this species should become extinct like so many others it had caused to disappear in its greed and its lust. If he let Monkey fly away with his solitary passenger, the remaining few souls on Earth would never escape the planet. In fact, they were now planning to annihilate each other even more completely if such a thing could be contemplated. Vith tried to explain this to Bertie, who was not prepared for the news.

"No!" he said, and then he said it again, *"No! No, no, nonononono—"* Bertie fell down on the ground and rolled in agony. He couldn't believe that after all the misery anyone could still think of fighting, yet it was true. Deep underground in a place like the one where the war had started, men were planning a second coming of death.

Earlier reports that both sides had expended all their weapons proved to be false. Over the next three years there were to be two more global skirmishes, each lasting about forty-five minutes.

"No! No, nonononono!" Bertie screamed. Vith observed his distraught pupil with compassion. For two days Bertie raved and babbled. During this time Vith considered the fate of humanity.

It was not supposed to have happened in this way. Vith was sent as an observer, to assess the damage and return to his own sphere with a report. He had arrived in the early 1950s, however, at the moment the race was amassing nuclear armaments and preparing to self-destruct. Now, after the war, he felt himself compelled to intervene.

No Daniel Webster appeared to plead the case for humanity. Bertie was insane over the idea of further warfare. The rest of the group at the camp were less advocates than innocent victims, sacrificial lambs caught in the bush. To be alone with his thoughts Vith withdrew from camp.

Rufus and Ben had become close friends over the weeks and months of their confinement. Together they stood watch over their tormented friend while his mind wrestled with the concept of more war.

"He hates to see peoples suffer, don' he?" Rufus said. "Don' he know yet they brings it on theyselves?"

"He knows. But his heart goes out to them, anyway." Ben adjusted the blanket over a shivering Bertie.

"Where Vith gone to?"

"I don't know," the tailor replied. "Maybe he went to bring Monkey back here."

"Yeah! Monkey, I'm goin' to have a word wit him. He supposed to be helping us. Instead he split!"

The children had accepted the idea that they would never again see their parents. Rufus had become a strong father figure for them, many of whom were ghetto kids. He was able to understand and soothe their basic anxieties. Camp had metamorphosed into a loosely structured school setting. Ben provided instruction in mathematics and the social sciences. Evenings found the whole camp seated around a giant bonfire, three or four kids in Rufus's enormous lap and others draped on his shoulders as they listened to Ben read from the gentler portions of the Old Testament.

> "Better one hand full and peace of mind than
> both fists full and toil that is chasing the wind."
> —Ecclesiastes 4:5–6

> "Clothed in majesty and splendour, and
> wrapped in a robe of light,
>   Thou hast spread out the heavens like a tent
>   And on their waters laid the beams of thy pavilion;

> Who takes the clouds for thy chariot,
> Riding on the wings of the wind."
> —Psalms 104:1–3

After two days Bertie stopped shouting *"No!"* and fell into a blissful sleep. Ben removed the restraints he had been forced to use and to which Bertie had reacted violently. If they had not tied him down, he would have hurt himself or someone else.

When Bertie awoke, he looked up into the concerned faces of Ben and Rufus and smiled. "Sorry, guys. I'm all right now. There's not going to be any long convalescence this time, no really, I'm okay." He was trying to get up, but they wouldn't let him. He lay back down. "Honest, I'm fine. I've worked it all out for myself."

"How's that?" Ben asked, sounding like a vaudeville straight man or Jack Webb on *Dragnet*.

"I can't save them. They can only save themselves. I did what I could."

"Right, Bertie. You done plenty. Look here at this place."

"Vith did this. But if this is all he can do, how can I expect to do more? It's up to him now. If he wants to save us, he can. Somehow we have to show him that we're worthy of it."

"He knows that already, Bertie." Ben explained that the real conflict for Vith was not their merits but the justice of his own actions. "In his culture, to interfere unwisely in the affairs of others, especially of other worlds, is one of the gravest acts."

"It's time now," said Rufus. He was right. Bertie fell back asleep while his two friends discussed the future in quiet voices.

Del and Bryce had taken a small cottage by the lake. Del's main contribution had been organic gardening, while Bryce

had teamed up with the tailor in making children's clothes
and in the care of the girls in the group, who now attended
her like so many little ladies-in-waiting. Bundled in a plough-
share quilt Del's grandmother had given her, one of the few
possessions she'd taken from her houseboat, Bryce sat up in
bed and recuperated from her ordeal while bright-eyed girls
brushed her hair and asked her what it was like to ride in a
spaceship.

"Was you afraid?" a cute Puerto Rican girl, Theresa, asked
her. Theresa was one of the fortunate ones whose lives had
been immeasurably improved by Bertie's random kidnap-
pings. She had been hungry since several months before she
was born, and she astonished the group with her appetite,
consuming bowl after bowl of the rich vegetable stews that
were a camp staple, along with hunks of the simple whole-
grain breads Bryce baked.

"Nah, I've been higher in a jet. I've even jumped from
higher up. Hey! Maybe you can learn to parachute with me,
if we ever get out of here."

"Where will we go?" her playmates wanted to know, and
Bryce couldn't answer them. They snuggled closer on the
bed and played with Bryce's old Raggedy Ann while Vith
decided their fate.

The evidence weighed heavily against mankind, he realized. If one considered the pristine perfection of the world
before man, how everything fit together so nicely and balanced so well, then observed the ravages of the recent war,
it appeared obvious that humanity was a lost cause. Their
vaunted scientific achievements had destroyed them. Only in
their religion and their art did men redeem themselves. Vith
had to keep reminding himself that his ancestors were the
interlopers who had engendered this catastrophe. This is what
swayed him, not any conviction that the race would change
but rather a sense of responsibility which, he realized, had
dictated all his actions on Earth.

"So be it!" he said to himself, sounding quite omnipotent. He laughed.

Up in H.M.S. (His Monkey's Ship) *Mahayana,* the defector from heaven had also decided that the time for action had come. Like the prodigal son, Monkey had never lost the shining soul of integrity that glowed within. He only needed to be prodded toward goodness. When _____ _____'s humiliation was complete, Monkey began to suffer the pricking pains of his own conscience. Rather than deprive an animal (which was how Monkey saw _____ _____) of natural companionship with its own kind, Monkey surrendered to his sense of duty and sought to bring his prisoner to Vith. Secretly he hoped for a reconciliation, for he knew he had behaved shamefully.

"I'm bringing you back to your own people, do with you what they may. How will you act when you no longer have the iron hand of Monkey at your neck? I don't know. You're just excess baggage on this all-monkey crew! Prepare to land." Monkey barked his orders. _____ _____ cowered in a corner, still in shock over the prospect of thirty years alone. When the giant ship settled next to the flagpole on the campground's central clearing, it was quickly surrounded by nervous Army men, who were experiencing momentary regret over their decision to give up their weapons to follow Vith. When the Great Teacher appeared, strolling into camp on foot, all fears were quieted. Everyone turned out except Bryce, who was afraid of _____ _____, and Del, who stayed by her side.

The spaceship door slid smoothly open, and Monkey appeared at the opening. Vith had walked right up to the ship to inspect it.

"Ah, there you are," he shouted at Vith, posturing as if he were a returning conqueror, for he planned to negotiate from a position of strength. "First—"

"First you will give me my cloud-seat, you little thief!"

"At once, at once, Great One." Monkey snapped his fingers, a very difficult feat only attainable by those with prehensile thumbs. The device appeared instantly.

"Next you turn over your prisoner to me."

"Of course, of course, Mahatma. It will be done." _____ _____ was dragged out by a dozen tiny brown hands. He fell to the ground in front of Vith, who had reinstalled himself on his cloud-throne.

"'Lo how the mighty have fallen!' Did you learn nothing from the ruination of your former realm?" Vith inquired gently, for in truth _____ _____ was reduced to a pitiful state. He feared for his life at the hands of his former victims.

"I don't care anymore," _____ _____ spat out, still defiant.

"You never cared—to your great detriment."

"What do you think of my ship?" Monkey pressed Vith, searching for a way to get back in his good graces.

"H.M.S. *Mahayana*. How appropriate. Can you accommodate more passengers?"

"I suppose so, if your Goodness requests it."

"I do."

"How many?" Monkey asked.

"All you see here."

"What?" Vith's announcement caused an uproar. He raised his hands for silence and received it at once, such was the respect he commanded.

"Some of you were in attendance at the Bronx Zoo. You knew then, and you others have since found out, that the world is in grave danger. That which I foresaw then has occurred."

Vith outlined the demise of the planet in terms that made clear the complete hopelessness of the situation.

"Because my ancestors were pernicious meddlers, I find myself obligated to repeat their errors. In order to cause the least possible disruption in the natural flow of things, I must

take you all, and this means you, too, _____ _____. To
the others I say that you must try to convert him to goodness.
Beware that he doesn't charm you into his ways, for his
tongue is smooth and his temptations are many."

The communion field hummed softly, modulating itself to
the various rhythms and tempos of the life-forms within its
range. Del and Bryce, munching on hash brownies in their
cottage, decided to make their stand.

"We'd like to stay," Del said, and though his words rattled
against the walls of the cabin like hail, everyone heard and
understood him.

"But, Del," Bertie cried, "you were the ones who most
wanted to travel in space!"

"Yeah, Bertie, buddy, that was *before* Vith showed us that
we're in space already. We like it right here. And anyways,
man, we can't leave now. We've got to stay here, with Vith's
permission—until Bryce has her baby, at least."

Vith nodded sagely. "These children of Bertie's will become the pioneers of the new world, for your journey is a
long and arduous one. Monkey, you have your orders. Get
to work!" The penitent ape jumped to the task with flair and
energy. He led his corps of monkeys into the ship, and soon
the busy sounds of construction and renovation were heard
within.

"Is there anyone else who wishes to remain behind?" Vith
continued. No one replied, but because Vith was so keenly
attuned to the sensitive vibrations of the communion field,
he heard the unuttered desire of one member of his congre-
gation. He chose to disregard it for the moment.

"Very well. Please don't be afraid of your fellow travelers.
Monkey and Cheetah you know already. The others Monkey
has brought along are all friendly fellows, just not so bright
as the two you've come to know. I'm going to collect a few
samples of this earth's plant life for your on-board gardens.
Please gather your belongings. Departure is imminent. Oh,

and if anyone hears a cock crow in the middle of the night, pay it no mind, it is only me." With these strange words Vith departed in his usual manner, so unobtrusively that it seemed a disappearing act.

Only by intuition did Bertie know that Vith's last words were a secret signal to him, for nothing had been said. The cock's crowing was his summons. At one o'clock that morning it came while everyone else in the camp slept their last night on Earth, under the familiar patterns of the constellations, the single moon traveling along its path across the horizon, the broad band of the Milky Way a silky swath viewed obliquely from this solar system's position on the edge of the spinning, galactic disk.

Bertie wandered out of his cabin and through the campground. In one cabin _____ _____ lay in an official Boy Scout sleeping bag, decorated with pictures of English setters at point. Relief flooded through him in a constant adrenaline rush, and he was already plotting seizure of the ship he hadn't even boarded yet. In another the Army captain and his squad had packed their gear and had held a short meeting at which they swore to uphold the principles of nonviolence with the same fervor they had once pledged to die bravely. They proved to be the most useful members of the spaceship, taking their orders from Monkey and performing the tasks of crewmen for whatever jobs the monkeys couldn't do. Because they were all young men except for the captain and would be forced into celibacy by their isolation, Vith made it plain to them that they were free to return to their homes and families, but most had none to go back to, and all were caught up in the importance of their new mission. Years later in their new home, a few would make May-December marriages with the grown-up children of the camp, but for most the decision to go meant a life of service, the libidinal energy rechanneled into fantastic accomplishments of pioneering.

Vith waited for Bertie by the lakeshore, where from a

quarter of a million miles away the playful moon caused the water to lap the sand with a harmonious white noise.

"I must be brief and direct. You wish to stay?"

"Yes," Bertie replied.

"Why?"

"I want to help those who are left behind, give them some hope, the ones for whom there is no hope."

"Aha, a bodhisattva. I thought so." And the trees sighed in the wind, and the eavesdropping animals cried out to each other: "A bodhisattva! A true Compassionate One! He will stay to help others when he could flee!" And they bowed down to Bertie and sang his praises in many animal tongues.

"By this act you show your true Enlightenment. There is nothing more I can teach you. I have withheld nothing. There is no secret teaching, no hidden meaning."

"What about the Book?" Bertie asked, though it no longer seemed to matter.

"The Book was a joke on you, a way to lead you and entice you to search farther, like the blank pages the clerics of Paradise gave to Tripitaka. But remember the moral of that story, in the immortal words of Buddha: 'It is such blank scrolls as these which are the true Scriptures. . . .' I have seen into your heart of Love, and it is very good."

"Yet . . ." said Bertie wistfully, unable to relinquish all at once the quest that had taken him so far.

"The Book was my way of putting things in a language you Americans would understand. It's nothing new, just a rehashing of basic Buddhist principles in the language of your culture. Everything changes, everything passes. If you had been other creatures, the words would have sounded differently, but the message would be the same."

Bertie winced to hear the Book belittled. "Couldn't I have a copy, anyway?" he asked, thinking of the future. "It might help me in my teaching."

"Very well."

The Book appeared in Bertie's hands, a brown tome decorated with living liquid gold letters: *TABOTD*. Bertie opened
it randomly to a section called the Book of Revelation. En-
tranced, he read the following passage while Vith slipped
away, never to be seen again by Bertie or any of the space
travelers.

> **I SAW THE WORLD TURNED TO FIRE.
> I SAW THE DEMONS OF FEAR AND IG-
> NORANCE BEING BORN FROM THE
> WOMB OF LUST. I SAW THE WORLD EN-
> SLAVED TO PIECES OF PAPER CALLED
> MONEY, EVEN WHEN THIS MONEY WAS
> TURNED INTO PLASTIC CARDS AND
> BUBBLES OF MEMORY IN MAGNETIC
> SUSPENSION. I SAW THEIR MINDS GONE
> SOFT AND FUZZY BEFORE THE GREEN,
> GLOWING, PHOSPHORUS VACUUM OF
> TELEVISION.**

> **THE DARK AGES RETURN! GOG AND
> MAGOG FEAST ON IDOLS OF CLAY,
> IDOLS OF IRON! IDOLS OF DOUBLE-
> SIDED DOUBLE-DENSITY SOFT-SECTOR
> VINYL!**

"This is amazing!" Bertie exclaimed, but the Universal
Magician was long gone.

The next morning, mist hung on the lake, ice-skating fair-
ies frozen in mid-swirl. The image of the spaceship was its
strangest reflection since a retreating glacier had created the
lake several thousand years previous. In a single evening the

monkey crew, together with the Army team, had refitted the rocket for human habitation, or rather cohabitation, with the active monkeys. Vith had made it clear that in the scheme of things he considered all animals to be equals and expected mutual respect from all concerned parties.

Early in the morning everybody met for breakfast in the big hall where Rufus, Ben, and Bertie had fixed a last breakfast of buckwheat cakes with honey, hash brown potatoes, orange juice, and coffee. Bertie revealed his decision to stay, and there was an outpouring of admiration, along with expressions of regret. The atmosphere was tense. Remembering the traumatic lift-offs of the early astronauts, people were expecting the rigor of g-forces, not the floating sensation they would get when they rose from the soft turf of the lakeshore. The children were awake early, like on a Christmas morning; they didn't have to be told that this was a special day.

Soon the time came for good-byes. Bertie stood next to the hatchway like a minister at the door of his church, shaking hands or hugging each entrant. Monkey, Ben, and Rufus were the last to enter, crowding the hatch like the Three Stooges while Bryce scattered wildflowers on the fuselage; on the nose cone Del smashed a precious bottle of Hans Kornell California champagne he'd been saving for a special occasion. It was, as far as he knew, the only bottle of Sehr-Trocken left in the world.

"The children—" Bertie started to say, but the looks from his three protectors told him that words were unnecessary, so all he could think to say was: "Have a nice trip." They laughed, and while they did, Bertie's eyes met Monkey's, and Monkey saw that he was dealing with a newly Enlightened One. "You behave yourself, Old Monkey," Bertie said.

"Yes, Great One," Monkey replied, using the same form of address he applied to Vith. "Perhaps I'll come back for you later."

"That's not necessary, but you could come to visit."

"All aboard," Monkey shouted. He wore a striped train engineer's hat that was startlingly incongruous for at least two obvious reasons, but the kids loved it.

Bertie, Del, and Bryce watched as the one and only colonizing mission set out to preserve the species *Homo sapiens*. The emigrants were like birds whose marshes had been drained, like the grizzly bears who had been driven north to the Arctic from their natural habitats, like any animals who had forsaken their homelands because of the intrusive and destructive ways of man. The ship lifted off without a sound, like a gas balloon, and for a long time Bertie could see the excited faces of his kids in the ship's windows, hear their noisy curiosity through the thin metal hull, as they drifted up toward the stars.

29

Dissolving into
the Boundless

"There is an allegory that depicts human life.
Once there was a man rowing a boat down a
river. Someone on the shore warned him,
'Stop rowing so gaily down the swift
current; there are rapids ahead and a
dangerous whirlpool, and there are
crocodiles and demons lying in wait in rocky
caverns. You will perish if you continue.'"

—from *The Teachings of Buddha*,
Bukkyo Dendo Kyokai

For the next forty-five years Bertie Rupp wandered across
the cremated landscape of America, armed with his copy of
the Book, preaching the gospel of love, compassion, and self-
determination. He survived World War IV and World War V,
each time returning to Vith's Pocono sanctuary where Del
and Bryce were raising the quadruplets from her first delivery.
After the third battle society ceased to function at a national

level. It became very dangerous to travel, as competing remnants of various factions sought control over the limited remaining resources. Still Bertie went from town to town with his message: the cause of suffering, the extinction of suffering, and the Path.

The land was full of prophets, doomsayers, eccentric mendicants of every persuasion, and people flocked to them with the desperation of drowning men, so it was easy for a real teacher like Bertie to accumulate a following after only a few days in any one place.

Once Bertie spoke to a great mass of people at the site of a town that had been leveled by conventional bombs and so was nonradioactive. It was on a fork of the Penobscot River in northern Maine, where refugees had fled from the attacks on Boston and the northeastern industrial corridor, at a place called Skattawumkeag, which in the language of the Penobscot Indian means "every wish fulfilled."

The people at Skattawumkeag were lucky: They had enough men with strength for work (elsewhere many suffered from the weakening effects of radiation poisoning) and enough building materials from the wreckage of the town that they could construct wooden shelters against the ferocious Maine winters. Bertie had visited many tent cities where all available wood had been incinerated for miles and miles around.

At Skattawumkeag Bertie gave his first famous sermon, of the group of speeches that have since been collected and annotated as an appendix or commentary on *TABOTD*.

Lifting the Book before him the way a rabbi holds the Torah, Bertie quieted the crowd. The only sound was the smooth-flowing wash of the river, icy-cold as always, but now also radioactive-hot.

"People!" Bertie would begin, "everyone here has lost someone in the last war. I myself lost many close friends and loved ones. What will we learn from this terrible tragedy? Will we rise up in the old cycle of revenge and cry for the blood of those who killed our families? Or will we finally admit that it is ourselves, our aggressions, our misdeeds that have led us to this meeting? Here is a river whose water you cannot drink. There is a town flattened to the ground, and yet we call it fortunate because it was bombed by high explosives instead of nuclear weapons. Listen, my friends, to these words, from the chapter entitled The Book of Atonement." As Bertie opened the Book he was amazed at how silent a crowd of four thousand people could be; there was scarcely a cough or a whisper.

"A FUNDAMENTAL LAW OF KARMA: NO DEPOSIT, NO RETURN."

After letting that precious extract of Truth seep into his listeners' minds, Bertie continued with a second reading:

"BIRTH GOES WITH DEATH. FORTUNE GOES WITH MISFORTUNE. BAD THINGS FOLLOW GOOD THINGS. MEN SHOULD REALIZE THIS: MINIMUM BALANCE REQUIRED."*

In this way Bertie elucidated the profound essence of knowledge as revealed in *TABOTD*. His fame spread by word of mouth until wherever he appeared, large crowds would gather to hear him. He acquired new disciples, including a biographer who transcribed his sermons. From time to time he withdrew for solitary spiritual retreat.

During one of those breaks from the rigors of foot travel and teaching, Bertie met a tired doctor who had sought solitude for the same reasons. Since each was seeking to be

Teachings of Buddha Bukkyo Dendo Kyokali p. 286.

alone, they approached each other warily when they met by chance. Each suspected the other of being a murderous bandit. It was very dangerous in these times to travel alone, especially where they were now, in the hills above a large city where Bertie had just finished preaching.

"Hello!" said Bertie. No one could mistrust him for too long. His aura was so pure, the light of his spirit so bright, that men came to believe in him after a moment's acquaintance.

"What are you doing up here?" the doctor asked him.

"I'm exhausted. I thought I'd find a field of hay to sleep in."

"Aren't you afraid of being attacked?"

"No," Bertie answered truthfully. "What about you? What are you doing here?"

"I'm a doctor. Believe it or not, I'm looking for herbs to grind up, for medicines, since there's no penicillin or tetracycline left in the state of Pennsylvania. You're that nut with the new religion, aren't you? I saw you in town. You should be ashamed of yourself, taking people's money for spreading those lies."

"I took no money and I told no lies." The doctor looked him over from a distance.

"All right, maybe you didn't, but it's damn hard to separate the truth from the bullshit, if you'll pardon my language."

"It always has been."

"You're right there. It's worse in my field. There's people running around all over peddling pills to cure the sickness when you know damn well there's not a functioning drug laboratory in the country. Most of those capsules have aspirin and baking soda in them—or worse."

"What is it you're looking for?" Bertie asked, and the doctor let go of his last suspicions and came over to Bertie. They sat on some rocks overlooking the city, untouched in the last war but reputed to be a target if there was a second strike, and so it had been abandoned by all but a few stubborn residents.

"Like every other doctor who's left, I'd like to find something that would combat the effects of the radiation. We had forty-some years and two hundred thousand cases to study after Hiroshima and Nagasaki, so you'd think we'd have come up with something." The doctor sounded bitter.

"What have you tried?"

"What haven't I tried? Sometimes I feel like a medieval doctor, dispensing my antimonies and calling in the barber-surgeon for amputations. Did you know that in the Middle Ages fungus from the skulls of executed criminals was administered as a powerful healing agent? Also powder of mummy, crushed body lice, and, of course, horn of unicorn."

"I have something you might try," Bertie offered.

"What's that?"

"It's a plant I found after it"—Bertie searched for a word to describe the transformation he had witnessed—"mutated. It's probably radioactive, but only at a very low level." Bertie reached into his pouch and withdrew the dried, pressed flowers of Emily. The doctor seized them with trembling hands, for by this time he had realized that he was in the presence of an unusual person.

"Very interesting. You say it's radioactive? Yes, maybe it would work like a vaccine, if I dosed them with it before they got too sick. I've got to run some tests on this. Will you excuse me?" The absentminded doctor was so excited by the prospect of a cure that he almost ran off before Bertie stopped him.

"Give me your address, will you? If it works, I'll get you some more."

"Where did you find it?"

"Kansas," Bertie answered.

"You can't get to Kansas. It's poisoned."

"I can get there." Bertie had no permanent address but

promised to stay in touch. The delirious doctor spoke to him three weeks later over a wireless set.

"Bertie! Bertie Rupp. You've done it. Get me all the flowers you can pick. I need them at once. I'm working on a synthetic, but it could take years. Please hurry."

Emily's name was forever linked to the curative drug made from her flower, and to Bertie's stature as teacher was added the honorific of miracle worker. The doctor provided Bertie with a good supply of the drug, which he gave out as he traveled.

As the years went by, Bertie's Enlightenment deepened. Like many teachers and priests, he grew in knowledge as he listened to people. He heard and saw a whole array of human life, and his compassion grew commensurate with his wisdom.

The legends of Bertie the Buddha are many and wonderful, but they cannot be chronicled here. This was the tale of Bertie's search for Enlightenment and the Book. Having achieved his supreme goal, Bertie renounced Nirvana for the task of saving the world and so became a bodhisattva. His forty-five years of service to humanity are the makings of another story.

A few days before his death at the age of eighty-two, Bertie completed a long trek to the Pennsylvania mountain retreat where the sons and daughters of Del and Bryce had founded an orphanage and monastery, under Bertie's direction. Bertie brought children to them from time to time, and many of his disciples remained there on a permanent basis, working at the orphanage when not in meditation. Handwritten transcriptions of portions of the Book were also undertaken, in the manner of monastic scribes of old.

Though he was now an old man, Bertie's eyes were clear, his grip firm. He was welcomed by the quadruplets, whom Del and Bryce had named after the four elements: the girls, Earth and Fire; the boys, Air and Water. They had spent the forty-five years of their existence in the tiny confines of the camp. The stories of Vith, Monkey, and the spaceship were like the Christ stories to early Christians, and Bertie was their St. Peter.

"Welcome, Master," Air addressed him adoringly.

"Just call me Bertie, please," said Bertie, but it was hopeless. They revered him.

"Yes, Master Bertie. How is Your Reverence?"

"I am tired."

"Come, we'll feed you, and then you can lie down. Later we want to show you some of the improvements we've made. We've added two barns since you were here last, and another dormitory. We're really booming."

"This will be my last visit," Bertie said simply. The Four Elements gathered around him protectively; they took his small travel bag from him and led him to the dining room where a feast had been laid out in his honor.

The next day Bertie gave his last sermon. His audience was composed of the Brotherhood of the Book, led by the Four Elements and the children of the orphanage. The monks numbered almost a hundred, the children more than two hundred. They all sat cross-legged in the sunshine, at the same spot where the H.M.S. *Mahayana* had alighted many years ago.

"The sight of you gathered before me is a blessing. I know that the teachings have not been in vain. All of you are familiar with the sacred legends of Vith, Monkey, and those few who have left this planet for new worlds. The fate of Earth we already know. But do not despair. By studying the Book and applying its moral lessons to our lives, we may be with them in their new homes, though we are far away. Yet if we ignore the Book, we will never be with them, even if we journeyed through space to join them.

"Don't depend on the Book alone. There are five thousand

volumes passed down over the last twenty-five hundred years which possess the essence of the same teachings.

"The Book is only one of many, and I am only one of many. Do not make a fuss over my death. Do not erect memorials to my name. I want to pass out of this existence 'like a snowflake dissolving in the pure air.'

"I urge you to live your lives firmly but gently. Listen to these positive words from the portion of the scripture known as the Book of Assurances:

IN THIS FOUNTAIN OF MYSTERY, SPIRIT IS ETERNALLY PRESENT IN END-LESS SUPPLY. ANYONE CAN AVAIL HIM-SELF OF IT FOR THE REFRESHMENT AND THE UNFOLDING GREATNESS OF HIS OWN SPIRIT BY THE EARNEST PRACTICE OF CONCENTRATION:*

NO ONE REFUSED

YOUR CREDIT GOOD HERE

ASSIGNED RISKS TAKEN

SE HABLA ESPAGNOL

Bertie spoke for a half hour, then he dismissed the children and lectured to the monks for another hour, quoting frequently from *TABOTD*, exhorting the brothers and sisters to search themselves for the keys to Enlightenment. At the end of his

---

*Tao Te King, Lao Tzu #6, from *A Buddhist Bible*, edited by Dwight Goddard.

speech Bertie retired alone to his cabin and died peacefully in his sleep.

Little more needs to be told. His corpse was cremated by his followers, and his ashes mixed with flour and fed to the birds, in the ancient Tibetan tradition. Do not think that some separate soul flew up out of his mortal body, for that would imply another incarnation, and Bertie was one of those who has gone beyond returning. Let it be said that he dissolved into the Boundless, becoming One with the All.

**THE POINT OF THESE TEACHINGS IS TO
CONTROL YOUR OWN MIND:
USE ONLY AS DIRECTED.**